What's Broken Between Us

Also by Alexis Bass

Love and Other Theories

What's Broken Between Us

ALEXIS BASS

HARPER TEEN
An imprint of HarperCollins Publishers

HarperTeen is an imprint of HarperCollins Publishers.

What's Broken Between Us
www.epicreads.com

Library of Congress Cataloging-in-Publication Data
Bass, Alexis.
   What's broken between us / Alexis Bass. — First edition.
    pages cm
   Summary: "A teenage girl must heal and learn to love again when her brother returns
from jail after causing a drunk driving accident that changed their lives forever"
— Provided by publisher.
   ISBN 978-0-06-227535-6 (hardback)
   [1. Dating (Social customs)—Fiction. 2. Brothers and sisters—Fiction. 3. Probation—
Fiction. 4. Family problems—Fiction. 5. High schools—Fiction. 6. Schools—Fiction.]
I. Title. II. Title: What is broken between us.
PZ7.B29255Wh 2015   2015005959
[Fic]—dc23   CIP
                                                                                             AC

Typography by Ellice M. Lee
15 16 17 18 19   CR/RRDH   10 9 8 7 6 5 4 3 2 1
❖
First Edition

For Dani and Ingrid,
who love each other no matter what

PJ: Tell us in your own words what happened that night.

JT: It was just a regular night . . . just another night out. And then, it turned into the worst night of my life.

PJ: It was the night of your high school graduation—so it wasn't really just another night, was it? You were celebrating.

JT: Oh, but we were always celebrating.

PJ: Tell me what you were up to that night.

JT: Well, going to parties. But you want me to say drinking, right? We were drinking, that's what we were up to.

PJ: You'd left one party and were headed to another when you crashed.

JT: That's right.

PJ: And the party you were on your way to was just six miles away . . . correct?

JT: Probably, yeah. You've got the facts, though, so I'll take your well-researched word for it.

PJ: Did you think, because it was so close, and in a part of town you'd grown up in and were so familiar with, that it didn't matter what state of mind you were in— that you'd be okay to drive that short distance?

JT: Sure.

PJ: It never occurred to you that you shouldn't be driving?

JT: No.

PJ: Did anyone at the party try to stop you? Or ask you if you were okay to be driving?

JT: Well . . . that's . . . that's sort of a bullshit question. I mean, no offense, but . . . have you even been to a party?

PJ: Explain it to us. To me.

JT: It's not a bunch of [expletive deleted] kids dancing to pop music, passing around hors d'oeuvres, playing charades—

PJ: Tell us what it's like.

JT: It's also not what you're thinking.

PJ: What am I thinking?

JT: That we're all . . . you know . . . half-naked, snorting blow off each other.

PJ: So what's it really like?

JT: It's like . . . we do whatever we want. But Grace didn't die at the party, did she?

PJ: Okay, I see your point, but—

JT: You definitely do *not* see my point. The party is not the problem.

PJ: People are dying every day at the hands of impaired drivers just trying to get to the next party. What would you say *is* the problem? Or better yet, the solution?

JT: I'm the problem. Me.

PJ: Have you spoken to the Marlamounts since the accident—have you had the chance to reach out to Grace's family?

JT: What do you think?

PJ: What did you say to them?

JT: Thank you.

PJ: Was that in response to their decision not to press charges against you?

JT: Mm-hmm.

PJ: And did you talk to them about Grace? What did you say?

JT: I'm sorry.

PJ: Grace wasn't the only one in the car. Your girlfriend was also in the car, and critically injured. Have you been in contact with her?

JT: Ex-girlfriend. I thought you had fact-checkers working at your fancy news station, Patricia.

PJ: You went your separate ways after the accident?

JT: Would you date me? Don't answer that. You're pretty attractive for a woman your age, you know.

PJ: I'll take that as a compliment and move on. What would you say to someone about to drive after consuming alcohol?

JT: I meant for you to take it as a compliment.

PJ: Jonathan.

JT: Patricia.

PJ: During your trial, your lawyers argued that there were additional factors that contributed to the accident. The roads were very wet, and a sign was missing from the highway warning about the curve in the road ahead. Do you think these factors affected your driving that night?

JT: I think many things contributed to the accident. My lawyers told me I couldn't say anything else.

PJ: You were given an extremely short sentence considering the crime, because of these reasons I've mentioned, and because the Marlamounts decided against pressing charges. There's been a lot of discussion in the media, including several articles published, about how a yearlong sentence doesn't fit the crime, despite these other conditions. How do you feel about your ruling?

JT: I feel exactly how you think I feel.

PJ: How is that?

JT: I'll be glad to get out as soon as I can. And maybe it makes me a horrible person, but whatever. There's a reason they call it an accident, you know.

PJ: The court called it vehicular manslaughter.

JT: Well, if you're going to get technical on me, Patricia. It's . . . it is what it is. . . . In here, or out of here—it doesn't change what I've done.

PJ: How are you going to cope with what's happened when you're released in a little under ten months? It will have been just over sixteen months after Grace's death.

JT: Oh, I'll probably just drink whiskey sours until I black out. I'm kidding. I just wanted to see you smile. It's your first smile since the camera started rolling, and it's such a great smile.

PJ: Sometimes when people smile, it's a defense mechanism. A way for them to cope with something they don't know how to deal with.

JT: I had no idea I had such an effect on you, Patricia.

PJ: The way you've behaved as we've conducted this interview . . . could it be you've put up a defense mechanism, too?

JT: Could be, could be. But if you're going to ask me if I feel remorse, the answer is: of course. [Muffled laughter.]

PJ: Do you find that funny?

JT: Oops, defense mechanism rears its ugly head.

PJ: Is there anything else you'd like to say about the accident? What would you say to someone about to drive after consuming alcohol?

JT: I'd like to say: Kids, remember the wise words of one Smokey the Bear: "Only you can prevent forest fires."

CHAPTER ONE

Grace Marlamount was the first one to die. I sort of wish I'd realized sooner, as early as when we all used to sit around in a circle at Stony Day Elementary, that we all had numbered days. Look to the left, look to the right. We're all going to die. But someone has to do it first. So who's it going to be?

And then maybe I would have paid more attention. Noticed more about the people I was spending so much time with, asked questions, been friendlier overall. Tried harder for a reputation outside of being Amanda, Jonathan Tart's little sister. Sometimes I wish for that.

Sometimes I think, *What's the use?*

The entire student body of Garfield High is here in the

gymnasium, all 582 of us, sitting shoulder to shoulder as Principal Green introduces a group dressed in red T-shirts and acid-washed jeans, standing in tiers, the A Cappellas for Change. They open with a rousing rendition of "We Are the World." There's a slide show on display on the right wall, flashes of kids our age who have all been cut out of existence because someone drove them off the road or into a tree or a freeway median or a pole after downing too many glasses of liquid courage. Though the lights haven't been dimmed, so we can hardly see the images.

The last few photos are of Grace; everyone cups their hands over their mouths in an echo of gasps. We all recognize her, even the freshmen and sophomores, who never went to school with her. This is the first real tragedy to strike our seemingly safe and boring, run-of-the-mill suburb since the early nineties—according to our parents. And thanks to my brother's national television debut on *Lifeline* and the flurry of articles that followed it, our sleepy town has turned into one of *those* suburban stories of *We Didn't See This Coming* and warnings of *This Can Happen Anywhere*.

"It's so sad," the girl in front of me says. She's a freshman, I'm guessing, because of the way she's declaring her grief, like she's not familiar with the way sorrow can bury you alive. She glances back at me. Since I've already made eye contact with her, I give her a small smile.

It's a practiced smile, as all my smiles now are, calculated and for other people's benefit. They are reassuring. *It's a shame,* my smiles say, *how the mighty have fallen.* They are sad, too, so people will know that I'm in pain for them, for Grace—an overcompensation sometimes, to make up for Jonathan not being here to grieve and apologize himself. My entire appearance is deliberate now. I can't look like I've just rolled out of bed and thrown my hair up. I wear mascara and lip gloss. Because when people look at me, they don't excuse what they see. Not anymore. Being Jonathan Tart's little sister used to give me a free pass for a lot of things—and ponytail hair is really the most trivial of them. Even the little things count now.

So I don't get to be sad however I want. At school especially, I have to be in the kind of mourning that apologizes.

The moderators from a group called Chicago Cares come to the stage next: a woman with a stern voice and a man who looks like he's about to cry. They spoke at an assembly last year, too.

"It's, like, best to hire a driver, I get it," someone jokes from behind me, and the result is a burst of hushed giggles.

"You lost one of your own in a drunk driving accident," the woman on the stage starts.

It sounds so generalized and cheesy, especially the second time around, but again, I feel my throat tighten up, and I have to suck on my lower lip to keep it from trembling.

"Grace Marlamount was supposed to be a senior this year," she continues. "She was supposed to be excited about the game on Friday, impatiently refreshing her email, waiting to hear back from colleges, thinking about what it was going to be like leaving home for the first time."

There's a long pause where everyone is actually quiet. I bow my head. Tears are brimming around the edges of my eyes, but I hold in my desire to sob. Crying is taking it too far. It might look like I'm laying it on thick, swimming in self-pity. Or worse, people could think I'm crying for Jonathan.

The truth is, even though we were the same age, I didn't really know Grace Marlamount that well when she died. Not the girl she'd become. Sutton Crane's partner in crime. The one who whispered the joke that triggered the loudest laugh in the room. The one yelling for my brother at the bottom of the stairs on a Saturday night—*Jon!A!Than!*—and who held the answer to the inevitable question, *What's going on this weekend?*

She was always magnificent—I remember that much—even before Jonathan declared it official. It's no surprise that she's the star of the homecoming assembly even more than a year after her death.

"Grace had her whole life ahead of her," the woman says, glancing back at the empty wall where the slide show had previously been playing. "And a single driver under the influence took it all away."

I exhale and try to collect myself now that she's brought up my brother.

The girls behind me whisper. *Grace was so nice*, they're saying.

This would be the part of the assembly where I'd turn to my best friend, Dawn, and we'd exchange a knowing glance, because that's exactly what Dawn and I used to say about her all the time, and though it sounds like a simple and small thing to say—*Grace was so nice*—when you're a pretty sophomore girl and your best friend is a senior, Sutton Crane, who's known for her sharp tongue, her ability to fill out a dress, and her charismatic boyfriend, you can be anything you want. Not everyone would have chosen nice. But Dawn's not here anymore; she's in college across the country. Another downfall of having an upper-classman as a best friend. If Grace were alive, maybe she'd be feeling like this, too—left behind.

It's ironic when you think about it, though I try not to, how the night of Jonathan and Sutton's graduation, Grace thought she was the one losing her best friends.

"You can't let this happen again," the woman says, her forehead pinching as her voice rises. "You all can prevent this."

The man takes over the mic with as much passion as his partner. "You all owe it to her. You have to promise. You have to be safer, smarter, more aware."

His eyes meet mine, but I think it's by mistake.

"You have to be the exact opposite of Jonathan Tart." Someone behind me says this, their voice cruel and bitter. The comment gets a few snickers, and again, I know these must be from underclassmen who don't remember the way Jonathan was worshiped. And that he was *so nice*, too.

It's been sixteen months since Grace died. Five months since Jonathan's *Lifeline* interview aired. Exactly three hundred and sixty-four days since Jonathan was locked up. And in twenty-four hours my brother will be getting out of jail. I don't *think* the man at the podium will bring this up, but I look at him for clues that he might decide the messy controversy about Jonathan's short sentence will help honor Grace.

"That's how you'll pay your respects to Grace Marlamount," he says. "By doing everything in your power to prevent this kind of reckless death in the future."

When the man and woman start to clap, the A Cappellas for Change group starts to clap, and then Principal Green joins in, so the rest of us do, too.

The starting string of the football team stands, preparing for the part of the assembly where all the fall sports teams are introduced. But everyone keeps applauding. I close my eyes and take a deep breath, and just like that, I've pulled it together.

CHAPTER
TWO

My days are numbered at Garfield High, and this, more than anything else, comforts me. I've made it through September and most of October. There are only 144 days to go.

One hundred and forty-four days of school after Jonathan has been released and will be living at my parents' house.

I plan to carry on how I always have since it happened, walking tall with my hair done and my clothes pressed, in adorable shoes that pinch. Smiling apologetically. Shaking my head whenever someone asks me about him, or the accident. That's where Graham Sicily will come in, blocking unwanted conversation.

"Wasn't it so emotional at the assembly this morning?"— Stacey Millbrant: fellow Stony Day Elementary survivor.

"Sometimes I think they need to show us photos of the car again; you know, something that will shock people more so they'll never forget. Especially for the freshmen."—Caleb Ruiz: self-proclaimed reformed pothead, who actually made T-shirts with *Don't Let the Party End Early* ironed across the front.

"Yeah, wasn't the car practically split in half? Did you see it, Amanda?"—Katie Easton: dance team captain; always wearing glitter.

Enter Graham Sicily. "Hey, you guys don't know why Trevor broke up with Leticia, do you? Everyone heard them screaming in the stairwell."

Graham is my boyfriend. It's really generous of him. He's getting the short end of the stick. He gets to date Jonathan Tart's baby sister right when it's no longer cool to be associated with Jonathan Tart. And I don't have sex with him. I blame it on my virginity, and on his, and a lot of times on a nonexistent migraine. But Graham is someone trustworthy. You can rely on him to change your flat tire. You can believe him when he makes a promise. He's good grades and good breeding and good fun. Graham Sicily is captain of the soccer team and student-council something—it always changes—and I'm fairly certain he's dating me because he feels like he's rescuing me, and he likes that feeling.

To be fair, most of the time he *is* rescuing me, warding off our shameless classmates who want to ask me about the details of the night Grace died, who are curious about how Jonathan's holding up in prison and want to talk about the unfairness of his sentence. Graham is there making excuses and ushering me away when I'm about to lose it, so no one ever has to see me fall apart and wonder if all my tears are for Jonathan.

"Try not to think about it," Graham says to me by my locker, a mere five seconds after successfully bringing up tomorrow's homecoming game to thwart another unpleasant conversation, this one comparing Jonathan to that kid who used affluenza to get off his murder charges—Graham's sixth rescue of the day, complete with a bit of advice. This is his solution much of the time. He used to put his hands on my shoulders, look deep into my eyes, and tell me, "None of this is your fault." Like he's watched that scene from *Good Will Hunting* one too many times. But I never mind.

Since it's Jonathan and his return on probation that's got me upset, Graham's new solution is to put it out of my thoughts. Don't think of him, because he doesn't deserve it.

"I'll try," I tell Graham, and he pulls me into a hug so huge and all-encompassing that I truly do feel safe in his arms, like I could dissolve here. I lean into him and pretend that I haven't just lied.

All I can think about is how the material on his soccer jersey would be perfect for catching tears. Graham knows I'm a mess, but he only knows the shallowest layers of the debris.

The truth is ugly, so I keep it from Graham, from everyone. Except Dawn.

The truth is: I'm glad my brother is coming home tomorrow. I'm *grateful* Jonathan's sentence was the minimum, one year in prison with ten years of probation. I understand that this is lenient, unfair, and not at all fitting to the crime. But the sentence makes me *happy*. Relieved, too. And it's not only because Jonathan has one of those faces that make people say, *He's too pretty for jail.* Or because I don't think he deserves to be there longer.

My brother was a shell of his former self after the accident. He didn't come out of his room. He barely got out of bed. His breath always stank of whiskey. He didn't speak.

So sometimes I can't bring myself to care that our team of the-best-of-the-best lawyers took full advantage of Grace's parents' refusal to press charges against my brother and milked the sign missing from the road and the haphazard weather conditions for all they were worth.

Jonathan killed one of his best friends. Nearly paralyzed his girlfriend. If that's not a life sentence, I don't know what is.

I miss being in my brother's shadow. It was warm there. But still, I'm afraid to see him.

I pull away from Graham and let him kiss me.

"What would I do without you?" I whisper. This compliment always brings out a candid, bashful smile in him, as though he can tell that I am actually being very genuine.

Graham gives my hand another squeeze before he leaves, walking in the opposite direction down the hall, and I make my way to my last class of the day, thanks to my open seventh period. It's such a relief. I stare at the floor as I enter the room, when a thought shadows over me. Dark and weighty and paralyzing.

None of this really matters. Not my secrets or the ways I try to apologize for Jonathan or even Jonathan getting out of jail tomorrow, because despite anything else that happens to me or Jonathan or the rest of us, Grace is still gone. So it's all useless anyway.

I'm standing in the doorway of my sixth-period Consumer Economics classroom, with no memory of walking there. I let my eyes travel to the other side of the room, where Henry Crane is sitting. He looks nothing like his sister, Sutton, otherwise you might say Jonathan and I had similar taste. But Henry is tan where Sutton is pale. His hair is a filthy blond, while hers is close to platinum. Henry's features are sharp; Sutton's are full. With Jonathan and Sutton, it had been love at first sight. It took Henry and me years to grow on each other. And we never got around to finding out if it was *love*. Henry is the person I try the hardest not to notice. I always fail. This time, he's actually looking back, staring at me like he can see the truth.

Texts to Dawn, Sent Thursday, 1:45 p.m.

I told you how we never talked about it, it just worked itself out—Henry takes the left side and I take the right. I get the window side of the classroom, and he gets to be closer to the door. But today he sat in the middle, just a desk away. So that's why I noticed he had a knee brace on, and then Bryan asked him if he'd be out this season and he said yes, for most of it, even though he was introduced with the rest of the soccer team at the assembly today. Then Bryan asked him how things

*were—in the broad sense—and Henry said, smashing.
And you know how whenever he plays on his accent he's
being sarcastic, but Bryan was like, okay, good to hear
it, man. Because that was probably the first time Bryan
and Henry had spoken all year, and then of course Bryan
turned to look at me because here he was, in between
Amanda Tart and Henry Crane, asking Henry if he was
okay in the broader sense, which was basically the same
as asking how he's doing with the fact that my brother will
be out of jail tomorrow, and all that.*

*And then Henry had Bryan pass me a note at the end
of class, which made Bryan turn red and frowny. I might
not open it, because is there anything he could say to me
that I'd want to hear anyway?*

*Damn, I didn't mean for this to be so long. Or to say
"which" so many times. Which means you should call me
the second you get out of Econ 101.*

That's right. I have your schedule memorized.

Which means I miss you like crazy.

CHAPTER
THREE

"That's all it said? 'Meet me after school'?" Just Dawn's voice over the phone grounds me. I no longer feel so lost.

I'm sitting in my car in the school parking lot, about to take off, except Dawn's class let out fifteen minutes before mine did and I couldn't wait another second to talk to her. I opened Henry's note as soon as I was alone in my car. Self-control failed and curiosity won, and there was a small voice in my head telling me that maybe, on some level, I owed it to Henry to open his note. And I definitely owed it to Sutton Crane, in case the contents of the note pertained to her.

"He didn't specify *where*?" Dawn asks.

He didn't, because he didn't have to. We had a place, as cheesy as that sounds. I never told Dawn about it.

"The point is," I say, "I have an open seventh period. I'm not going to wait around after school, when I don't need to be here, just so he can—"

But I'm cut off by a knocking on the passenger window. It's him, of course, standing there in his jacket, leaning over and motioning for me to press the button to lower the window.

"I have to go," I whisper to Dawn, hanging up on her mid "Wha—?"

Henry stands upright as the window descends, and once it's all the way down, he reaches into the car, unlocks it, and climbs into the passenger seat. His gesturing from before might've been asking me to unlock the door. Our miscommunication is no surprise.

It's been over a year since we've spoken, so I wait for him to start. The last thing we said to each other, *Let's just forget it*, was the same as agreeing never to talk again. In theory, it was easy to keep this agreement, since our mutual friends are nearly nonexistent now that Grace is gone and his sister and my brother have been separated by miles and metal bars.

"I didn't think you'd meet me," he says quietly. His eyes drop on my keys, resting firmly in the ignition. His subtle way of saying, *And I was right*.

"I—I have an open seventh," I explain.

He takes up a lot of room in the car, like maybe he's taller. Up close he looks the same. His hair is a little shorter, like he just got it cut. It's still sort of wavy, still falls uneven over his forehead. I remember touching it, and wish I didn't.

"Can I ask you something, Amanda?" he says.

Sometimes when he says my name it comes out *Amander*. It stuns me for a second, hearing him say my name. His family moved from England when he was twelve and Sutton was fourteen, though I think Henry works hard to keep his accent strong because girls like it. I used to be the exception, but then, for a moment in time, I was worse than all of them. At least for me, it was more of an acquired taste.

"A favor," he says, staring straight ahead. "I need a favor."

"What's the favor?" I ask, but this feels all wrong.

I should be asking Henry how his sister is doing, that's what I should be saying to him after not speaking to him for a year, but I can't bring myself to mention her. It's bad enough that my brother's the reason Sutton spent the first year after her graduation, when she was supposed to be attending the Art Institute of Chicago, in and out of physical therapists' offices. Last I heard she was walking again but could only do it with crutches attached to her forearms. I'd like to know if she's doing better, if she's in the city studying fashion like she always wanted, even though my brother wasn't around to go to school in the city with her the way they'd planned it. But I know better than to ask. Because the answer could be no.

"He gets out tomorrow?" Henry says, though my brother's release is probably a big point of discussion in the Crane household, and Henry most likely has had that date burned into his memory from the moment the trial was over.

"It is what it is, I guess," I say, immediately regretting the words, but I felt like I had to say something. I never was good at offering condolences, and my apology-smile won't work on Henry.

Henry looks at me, finally. I hadn't realized how intently I'd been waiting for him to meet my eyes, but now that he has, I feel a mixture of sorrow and relief.

Henry covers his mouth, then quickly moves his hand away. "You sound just like him," he says.

It's . . . it is what it is. . . . In here, or out of here—it doesn't change what I've done.

"I didn't mean to—"

"I know, I know. I shouldn't have said that. I don't know why I thought it was okay to rouse you about talking like him."

There was a time when Henry and I were sparring cronies. Nemeses. It started in junior high. Then Jonathan and Sutton fell in love and I was irksome and Henry was disgruntled, and our game was to pretend our siblings weren't exchanging saliva and calling each other *baby.* At the height of our gaming, though, the verbal scrapping started to feel a lot like flirting. And soon it was impossible to deny that we were dancing around our feelings for each other, and so we decided to just fess up to them.

"Maybe it's your defense mechanism," I say. Henry started it. I can't help myself. It's what we do—what we used to do. Or maybe I'm the worst, plain and simple, and it's no wonder I don't have any friends my senior year.

Henry raises his eyebrows. A look of challenge, of surprise. But not offense. He never did get offended.

"So what's the favor?" I ask again. I'm sure it's evident by my expression: whatever it is, I'll do it. If it will absolve me in any way, for everything before, for what Jonathan's done, and said, and for this conversation right now, sign me up.

"If you happen to notice that he's back in touch with Sutton, I need you to tell me. Will you?" Henry chews his bottom lip, waiting for my answer.

"Sure." He does nothing to hide that he's scrutinizing me. "*What?*" I ask.

"You tell me."

I let my mouth hang open, but he's right. I do have a *what*.

"On *Lifeline* he said they weren't speaking." I realize what a huge mistake it was to mention *Lifeline*, and usually I don't, but the thing is, I haven't spoken to my brother—not a word—since he was incarcerated, per his wishes. The reminder makes me want to start crying. It takes me back to that foggy Thanksgiving Day last year, when I thought we'd make the drive and visit him, since it was a holiday. But my parents ignored my request. I was drowned out by football on the television, and my mother's bedroom door, slamming closed. I had to realize by myself that when Jonathan said he wasn't going to list us as visitors, he meant it.

"On *Lifeline* . . ." Henry twists to look at me. His face is a giant question mark, and I almost ask *him* "What?" but he's shaking his head, leaning back in the seat, staring out the windshield instead of into my eyes. "If you believe anything he said on

Lifeline, well . . . I don't know what to say to you."

The lawyers told us, "People aren't themselves in front of a camera," after the interview aired and my parents and I were in shock about my brother's performance. But Jonathan was exactly himself in that interview, the boy he was before the accident. Cheerful. Smug. Inappropriate. Flirtatious. Relaxed, like he didn't have a care in the world. My parents and I cling to the words *defense mechanism* tighter than we've held on to anything in our entire lives.

Lifeline is all I have to go on; it's all anyone has. That's the problem. It never occurred to me—until now—that Jonathan never went to see Sutton in the hospital once during those months before his incarceration, and therefore what he said on *Lifeline* is what she gets instead of a real breakup. It's all we have of my brother, and Henry thinks it's a lie.

"How do you know he was lying?"

"Because it's what he does!" Henry explodes. There's fire in his eyes, and in his voice. "Televised or not. In front of a jury or not. He said he's not speaking to Sutton, so naturally I assume they must be talking every day." Henry swallows down the flames, and his stare turns to ice. "Or they will be, after tomorrow."

I'm about to ask Henry why he doesn't just question Sutton about whether she's in contact with Jonathan. But I already know the answer. Sutton doesn't tell the truth either.

"Okay, fine," I say. I hope this will get him to leave. I prefer undeserved glances across a classroom, silence for the rest of our lives, if it means never having to be around him when he's mad like this. This is the kind of fighting we never wanted to do—it's the reason we had to forget everything that was happening between us. And really, I'm mad, too. But my fury is defenseless. I don't get to tell anyone they're wrong about Jonathan, especially not Sutton's younger brother. "I'll tell you if I hear anything."

"Thank you," Henry says in a callous voice. He stays perfectly still.

"She probably doesn't want to talk to him anyway," I say, a moment later, as an afterthought. But even I can think of a million things Sutton undoubtedly wants to say to Jonathan.

I wait for Henry to yell at me for this, too, but he shakes his head. "It's not always that easy." He happens to glance at me at the exact same time I glance at him, and then he's opening the door and walking away, and as I'm watching him go, I stupidly wish that he would come back.

CHAPTER FOUR

There are a handful of people who seemingly have nothing better to do on a Friday afternoon than sit outside the federal prison in rusty folding lawn chairs, holding signs. Mostly, the signs say things like NO JUSTICE FOR GRACE MARLAMOUNT! and RETRIAL! That's the gist of what they're chanting.

I didn't have to go with my parents to pick Jonathan up from prison. I'm missing a calculus test, but if I'm going to be ratting Jonathan out for speaking to his ex-girlfriend, being here when he's released so he doesn't have to sit there by himself with our parents the entire five-hour drive back is the least I can do.

The windows of my parents' SUV are slightly tinted, but I still find myself slouching in my seat. No one from Garfield

High is protesting, from what I can tell. No one representing a religious sect, either. It's just a few middle-aged people—*Lifeline* demographic, aka people who like to spend their Friday nights on the couch tuning into the grandest, most elaborate dramatization of news stories. One sign misspells Jonathan's name: JOHNATHAN. You'd think if they cared enough, they'd get it right. One of the cars has an Arkansas license plate, and I wonder if that drive through Missouri was really worth it to stand here on the side of the road in the cold, shouting at strangers.

The lawyers warned us that Jonathan's interview might "complicate things for him at the time of his release." I wonder if this is the worst of it.

"This is unbelievable," my mother mutters from the front seat. She's got on her large black sunglasses with a red silk scarf hooded around her head. She's clutching her purse on her lap like she thinks someone is going to reach out and grab it. Her mouth—the only part of her face I can really see—goes slack. I lean forward and touch her shoulder, giving her a weak smile. Under normal circumstances, I don't touch her and she doesn't touch me, but my mother is at a federal prison picking up her only son, whom she hasn't seen or spoken to in a year. She breathes out and pats my hand. "I just want to get this over with." Her voice is high and muffled from crying.

"It'll be all right," my father says. It's the only thing he ever says regarding this entire situation. "Just ignore them. They have their own problems, I'm sure."

My father is full of empty advice. This kind of encouragement might work on his patients prior to dental surgery, but has never worked on us. My mother sighs.

We follow the road down a little ways and park beside a white Pinto in a small, nearly empty lot.

My mother leans forward, focusing on the dusty blue doors of the cement building in front of us.

"What are we supposed to do now? Do we just sit here and wait? Do we need to go in and—" A buzzing noise cuts her off, and one of the hefty doors slides open. A guard dressed in tan holds it as my brother and another boy walk out.

"Here he comes," my father announces. My mother gasps. Like me, she's now holding her breath.

Jonathan stares at his feet while he walks. He's missing his usual saunter. His dark hair seems thicker, but I think it's because I've never seen it so short before. Usually it covers his entire forehead and wings out at his ears. He's in jeans and a sweatshirt—the clothes he was wearing when we brought him. They're baggy on him now, and when he finally does look up, all his features are sharper. He's only nineteen, but he seems older. In some ways he's the same as when we brought him here a year ago—broken, sad, guilty. Those things are now etched into his creased forehead, looming behind his eyes.

He veers to the left as he's walking, and at first I think it's an accident, he's done it to prevent himself from tripping. But he falls in step with the other boy, who was let out of the door right before Jonathan. Talking with his head down, Jonathan makes this boy laugh. And then we see it, a real live smile from my brother. It's small, but it's there, it's genuine. It's him.

The two of them exchange a half handshake, half hug before the boy climbs into the white car that is there for him, and suddenly all I can see is my brother. Not a prisoner. Not a sociopath. Not a murderer.

I'm grinning so big my cheeks shake. Any second my eyes are going to spill huge tears of happiness. I had no idea it would be like this.

"Don't get out of the car, Amanda," my mother says, but it's too late. I open the door and watch as my brother's eyes widen when he sees me. I think he's going to cry, but he surprises me for the millionth time. When I reach him, he throws his arms around me and I bury my face in his shirt.

He's slow to pull away, and when I look up at him, I see that he's staring straight ahead through the windshield at my mother. Her French-tipped nails disappear under her sunglasses as she tries to wipe her eyes. Jonathan walks calmly to the other side of the SUV and opens the door. He leans toward her, taking her sunglasses off and hanging them on the collar of his T-shirt. She cries and he watches. When he hugs her, he bends over her, so she doesn't have to move or even take off her seat belt. With her purse still between them on her lap, she sobs on Jonathan's shoulder. He puts a hand over the scarf around her head and whispers something in her ear that makes her cry harder. I think that she might be crying now because she's happy. Maybe she doesn't know what else to do.

With my mother's sunglasses still dangling from his shirt,

Jonathan slides into the backseat, and we pull out of the prison parking lot. Jonathan lowers the window to wave once more at the boy who climbed into the white car.

"Who was that?" my mother asks, turning her head a bit so she can see Jonathan. Judging by the tone of her voice, you'd never know that seconds ago she was a blubbering mess. "What did he do to get in there?"

Not once have I heard my mother say the words *jail* or *prison*. It's always *that place* or *there*.

"Mike, drug dealer," Jonathan says. "I mean, Mike, *reformed* drug dealer."

If my brother didn't look like he needed ten cheeseburgers and ten hours of sleep, I might've teased him about making new friends. It used to be that Jonathan would get in trouble and we'd laugh about it. The desire to make him smile right now is so strong I don't trust myself with words at all.

My father takes this moment to acknowledge Jonathan. "So, how are you, son?"

"As well as can be expected." Jonathan stares out the window. "I'm here with you all, so I'm much, much better now."

"What's wrong?" my mother asks, her voice panicked as if he didn't just tell her he was doing *better*.

Jonathan glances her way, then very quickly looks out the window again. But I saw his expression for that brief moment. It's a face from before Grace died. It said, *You're joking, right?*

"You think prison had an effect on your . . . on Mike?" my dad says, peeking at Jonathan in the rearview mirror.

My mother sighs, annoyed and showboating it, the way she does whenever my father says something she doesn't approve of.

"Sure," Jonathan says, shrugging.

As we approach the prison parking lot exit, my mother says, "Just ignore them. They're a bunch of assholes with nothing else to do." My mother doesn't look like the type to curse; she comes off too proper, too uptight. But she does it a lot as long as she's not in public. Wiggling her fingers, she reaches back toward Jonathan. He gets her signal and gives her back her sunglasses.

"Celebrity has its price." Jonathan's voice is dry and humorless and aching. But he leans forward toward the center console, so he can get a full view of the protesters through the front windshield.

They seem more aggressive now that we're leaving the prison; like they're very aware it's possible that one of the exiting cars could contain Jonathan.

I let my hand hover over the button in my door, fantasizing about what it would be like to lower my window and tell them they make everything worse. I feel Jonathan's hand brush past my wrist, like he can't decide between tapping my palm or grabbing my hand.

"It's fine," he whispers to me.

I shake my head, *it's not*, but he's turned around, watching as the protesters fade behind us. Jonathan choosing to stare at the protesters reminds me of when he used to sit too close to the television, even though he'd get yelled at for it. The second our mother left the room, he'd scoot his gaming chair right up to the

TV and press his feet into the bottom drawer of the TV stand. His eyes would be wide and bleary and watering. But he didn't care. He didn't want to do what was good for him, no matter how simple it was.

CHAPTER
FIVE

Jonathan used to regularly wake me up on Saturday mornings, usually at three or four a.m., when he'd be getting home from a party. Typically he'd be with Sutton and Grace, and I'd hear the closing of doors, footsteps on the hardwood, beeping from the microwave, or the sound of laughter, and I'd wake up.

This Saturday morning I wake up at five a.m.

I'm uncharacteristically starving—or maybe I'm always this hungry at five a.m., but am usually too asleep to notice. The English muffins sitting in our cupboard aren't going to cut it, and it seems unnatural to be awake this early without any caffeine. I pull a sweatshirt over my tank top and redo my ponytail, figuring that's good enough, as it's probably too early to be running into someone I know.

I clomp down the stairs in my slippers, regretting so much that I didn't put my car in the garage last night and now have to deal with the early-morning chill factor. I'm wrestling my coat out of the closet when I spot Jonathan sitting by the window in the living room.

"You're awake," I say. A surprise, considering the first thing he did yesterday upon returning home, after eating a cheese-burger like it was his last meal, was head up to his room and lock the door. My initial thought was that he must still have some whiskey hidden in there somewhere. I went upstairs at eleven and I could hear the television on in his room. And when I ran into him in the hallway as he was making his way to the bath-room, his eyes were red and he walked like he was trudging through sand.

Jonathan jerks his head at my voice, as if even though I sounded like an angry elephant coming down the stairs, he was too entranced gazing outside through the lace curtains to notice.

"You're one to talk."

"I was just going to Starbucks," I tell him. "For coffee." My stomach gurgles. "And a sandwich."

"Coffee would be amazing," Jonathan says, staring into the mug he's holding. It probably contains coffee, but because our parents make their own coffee only when guests are here, I'm betting the coffee grounds are very old. Plus, Jonathan is like me. He says coffee, but what he means is "caffeinated flavored bever-age masking the taste of coffee."

"Want me to bring you back something?"

"Please." He brings the cup to his lips, but he can't seem to make himself drink. I don't blame him.

"What are you in the mood for?"

"Just get me whatever you get." Jonathan's current smile is a depressed version of his regular smile.

"Hey," I say. "Do you want to come with me?" I don't add that it's so early we probably won't see any people we know.

"Are you sure?"

He's out of his room. He's awake. His eyes are clear.

I reach into the closet for his jacket and toss it at him. It lands barely a few feet from me, right where the edge of hardwood in the foyer meets the creamy carpet of the living room.

"I see nothing has changed with you," he says.

I chuckle as he comes forward to retrieve his coat. Everything has changed with me. Everything. But maybe not this, not us.

Starbucks isn't crowded, but there are five more people here than I'd expected so early on a Saturday morning. Mostly older people who were probably in bed by six. There's a woman bouncing with a newborn swaddled against her body. Every time she stops bouncing, the baby turns red and lets out a scream. She's having her coffee standing up. Before, Jonathan would have said something to make her laugh. Not just because she was a pretty girl, either. But because she could so obviously use a fleeting moment that allowed her to forget she was on her tenth day of no sleep. He was always good at distracting people.

Now he keeps his head down. His coat is so big it practically swallows him. He could slouch and his head would disappear like a turtle. I order us peppermint mochas and breakfast sandwiches to go, and we take a seat at a table in the corner while we wait.

"Peppermint mocha?" Jonathan says. "I thought those were only available around the holidays."

"A common misconception."

He cringes. I'm about to ask him what's wrong, but he speaks again quickly.

"I can't believe I left you alone with them on Christmas," he says, looking down. "I'm so sorry." He continues before I can tell him it's okay. "How bad was it?"

"Oh, our parents." I give him my best reassuring smile. He squints slightly, like he knows this isn't my usual look. The truth is we barely acknowledged Christmas last year. There were no sweaters. No eggnog. Definitely no holiday party. My parents, who usually live for country-club-sponsored events, avoided the club for fear that they might be forced to discuss what they usually refer to in front of their friends as their "legal woes." I was glad I didn't have to endure the usual brand of torture—being paraded around like some sort of mascot to parties where everyone was trying to out-holiday everyone else and family togetherness came with a scoreboard. We didn't even bother with a tree last year. Just lights strung up on the outside of the house, so to anyone passing by, it'd look like nothing was wrong. We exchanged gifts over hot chocolate on Christmas morning, but the only thing familiar about Christmas was the presents, all wrapped in the same silver paper the volunteers at the mall use.

"I'll make it up to you," he says.

His eyes are so sad. And no matter how foreign the rest of him is now, despair has always looked especially alien on him.

"We were too busy for Christmas," I say. "I was worried about the SATs. Dad took on all of Dr. Halberstein's old clients. Mumsy was—" This is what Jonathan and I call our mother behind her back. To be honest, I doubt she'd mind if we called her that to her face, until she realized we didn't mean it as a compliment.

"Mumsy," Jonathan finishes the sentence the only way it really can be finished. *Mumsy was Mumsy.* She was in jail, too. It was happening to her. It was too much. There was no time for Christmas.

"All the things we hate didn't happen this year." I'm trying to get him to see the silver lining.

He searches my face, like he knows I'm not telling him the whole story.

"You're off the hook," I say.

He ignores this, looking away.

"So how's school?" Jonathan says after too many beats of silence.

For some reason, I think this might be his way of bringing up Grace.

"Sorry," he continues. "I didn't mean to sound like Standard Dad." Standard Dad is what I call our dad. He isn't really a "standard dad" with Jonathan—he's looser, and he doesn't sound like he's reading from a manual (which I claim is called *The Manual for Standard Dads*). Jonathan would sometimes tell me to give him a break. But then our dad would say something to me like, "Atta girl" or "Keep your eye on the prize," and Jonathan and I would look at each other, my point sinking in, his argument irrelevant.

"Have you talked to anyone from school?" I ask. My voice is shriller than normal. "Or . . . anyone else?"

"Nope," he says slowly. Jonathan severed ties with all his old friends after the accident. I'm sure it was pretty effortless—I don't think any of them tried reaching out to him, and if they did, his *Lifeline* interview probably chased them away for good. He shifts uncomfortably in his chair, like he knows this is my way of asking about Sutton.

"I'm not taking calls right now," he says. "Or making them. I'm not participating in telecommunications whatsoever at this moment in my life."

"That's . . ." I have no idea how to finish. "Convenient."

A barista with dark hair piled on top of her head comes over to our table, holding both our coffees. Our breakfast sandwiches are pinched between her elbow and her side. "Amanda, right?"

"Uh . . . yeah." One hundred percent of the time, in my experience, the baristas at Starbucks shout out your name. They aren't in the business of delivering your food right to you.

"Here you go," she says. She sets the food down in front of us, while snapping her gum—surely breaking what I assume is another rule in coffee service. Her dazzling, albeit tired, green eyes are fixed on Jonathan. This isn't something new—girls staring at him. It's just different now.

"I recognize you," she says.

Jonathan and I exchange a glance. I scoop up the breakfast sandwiches, ready to storm out the door before this girl can begin her tirade about justice.

"I recognize your eyes," she says. "They're so beautiful."

Jonathan looks at me again, confusion softening his expression. Our whole family has brown hair, but Jonathan inherited my mother's blue eyes. My eyes were blue when I was born, then turned brown when I was four months old. There are exactly eight pictures in existence, taken before they changed, in which my brother and I actually look like we belong to the same family.

"Thank you," he says very quietly.

"They make an impression," she continues. "You . . ." The girl puts her hands in her apron pockets, looking down at them as though this will make her smile invisible. "You *made* an impression."

I've still got the sandwiches in my hand, my coffee two inches off the table. She seems harmless, but I can't trust her. Even while she's wearing that smile my brother was always good for.

"I've wanted to meet you." She takes the empty seat next to my brother, sitting backward in the chair, crossing her arms over the top of the backrest. Jonathan leans away from her. He keeps glancing at me, like he's waiting for my cue. But I'm waiting for his—too shocked to come up with one of my own.

"You were really fucking honest," she says. "Like, no bullshit, this is what you think—don't blame the party, people are the problem. People are morons, people are idiots."

Jonathan clears his throat. "I said *I* was the problem."

"Exactly." She sets her hand on the table, spreading her fingers so she almost touches the base of Jonathan's coffee. "No one is ever fucking honest."

My brother relaxes in his chair; his coat puffs up in front as he leans back. "Thank you." It comes out unsure and hesitant. Both things my brother has never been before.

"I'm Wren," she says, holding out her hand.

"Jonathan. And this is my sister, Amanda."

Wren smiles at me but doesn't bother shaking my hand.

"I'm on my break—you want a smoke?" she says to him. "You seem like you could use one."

"I'm set, thanks," he tells her.

"Maybe you'll look normal again once you get some nicotine in your system." Something I've accidentally learned about flirting is that sometimes, when you say something mean about someone's appearance, it's actually an indication you're really, really into them. I try to imagine how Jonathan must look now to someone who doesn't know that his clothes don't usually hang off his hips and his skin isn't usually this pale. Wren bites her lip as she stares at him, and it's so intimate that I feel intrusive watching.

"Smoking is the one vice I do not have," he tells her. This wasn't true last year, but I guess it is now.

"Okay, sure," she says. "Why don't you keep me company and I'll see how well that story holds up?"

Jonathan moves to stand. "We've got to get going. But maybe next time."

We walk out the door before Wren can get clarification on "next time."

"So, she was sweet," I say on our way home.

I'm kidding, but Jonathan still says, "No, she wasn't."

"That's never been your type, anyway."

"No, it hasn't."

It's the closest we've come to talking about Sutton since the accident.

Most of the time, I try not to think about what happened the night of the accident.

It's easier to think about what I wish would have happened. I barter moments. Recast everything.

I move the graduation party from Sylvia Bickerstaff's to Calvin McKay's, because they say that his parties are stocked to last all night long.

I change my response when Jonathan yelled, "Baby sister! I'm a graduate!" from across the room. Instead of rolling my eyes, blowing him a kiss, and giving him a smile before quickly leaving the room, I forget what I'm waiting for—who I'm waiting for—and go over to him. I play along. I humor him and pretend we didn't have this same interaction a few hours before.

I tease him right in front of Sutton about the fedora and

matching blazer he's wearing, even though they were her doing and she's pinching her lips together as she glares at me.

I stay close to him, complaining about how Dawn's ignoring me to make out with Blake Highlander. That actually did happen, Dawn and Blake. It was the night she lost her virginity. I wouldn't change that. It works that I'm alone. Jonathan wouldn't have wanted to desert me at the party.

I put Graham at the party, too. He looks the way he often did when we were sophomores, shoulders back, wearing a sideways smile, head constantly bobbing—trying too hard. He turns it on for Grace, for Jonathan, because deep down he's just like everyone else; he cares about impressing them.

My brother decides Graham is worth adopting for the night. Sutton nudges Grace, moving her eyebrows up and down, whispering, "He's dreamy for a jock." And Grace doesn't want to leave Graham's side. Graham feels the same way, because though he can't make sense of it, he knows that he is somehow rescuing her. Grace disappears with him somewhere in Calvin's house, so when Jonathan and Sutton turn drunk in the way that makes them handsy and sleepy, she's somewhere else, perfectly entertained.

I change Henry's answer to my text. It says that no, he can't leave Matt's party. But he wants to see me later, another night, just the two of us. And he admits, *I can't stop thinking about you.* That's enough to temper my disappointment.

I relax the rest of the party, let myself get sucked into the couch, and even find comfort in my brother's usual antics. We don't leave until the sun's coming up, catching a ride on the first bus of the day. The driver laughs as Sutton dances in the aisle with Grace after Jonathan talks him into turning on the radio.

When I finally do go to sleep, I have good dreams about what it'll be like meeting up with Henry the next day. And I wake up to the sound of my brother's voice: *Get out of bed, baby sister. I'm a graduate and we're still celebrating.*

There's a simpler change, of course, if I could go back. One where I'd get to keep all the good things about the night.

Just take away his keys.

One swipe in his pocket—*got 'em!*—that's all that really had to change.

It's the simplest answer. It's also the most unrealistic.

CHAPTER
SIX

*H*omecoming is a lot more than just a dance. I didn't know this, but Mumsy readily informs me when we run into each other in the kitchen around noon and she asks me what I'm up to tonight. I tell her that later this evening I will be accompanying my boyfriend, Graham Sicily—in case she's forgotten about him—to the homecoming dance.

"That's tonight?" she stammers. "And you haven't started getting ready yet?"

Luckily for me, she's able to squeeze me in at her salon with a new girl who is looking to gain clients. The end result is my hair transformed into a tornado of curls, held together with so much hair spray I think my hair might stay like this through the end of the month.

I'll pick you up at 6:30, k? Graham's last text reads.

OKAY, I text back, using all caps to convey enthusiasm.

But Graham's next text is, Are you mad?

NO, EXCITED.

Digital communication is such a problem sometimes.

Graham arrives, punctual as ever. He comes in and his eyes give him away. A glance to the stairs, down to the floor, toward the living room, back down to the floor. He's looking for Jonathan.

Mumsy is the first to make an appearance, followed by Standard Dad in tow with a camera. "That dress is very orange." She blinks rapidly. She does the same thing when she eats something too spicy.

I agree with her, but the salesgirl told me it was the color of the season. That's why I bought it. Doesn't everyone want to be the girl wearing the color of the season?

"You don't like it?"

"It fits you perfectly." Still blinking rapidly. She pulls her cashmere wrap tighter around her. *She can feel her own glacial freeze,* Jonathan used to say.

"My little girl looks so beautiful!" Cite *The Manual for Standard Dads,* page 89, chapter 4: "Milestones."

He gives me a hug.

"Jonathan!" my mother yells up the stairs. Standard Dad has already started snapping photos. "Are you going to see your sister off?"

"I can't believe how fast you've grown up." Cite *The Manual for Standard Dads*, page 4, chapter 1: "Generalities."

Jonathan comes down the stairs slowly. He's swimming in his favorite sweats, worn and gray, with *Chicago Bulls* written down the side of the left leg. His eyes are puffy, and everything about him is droopy as he stands on the last step, leaning against the wall. I think he might be drunk. But part of me wonders if maybe he's just sad.

"Hey, man." Jonathan barely nods at Graham, barely makes eye contact with him.

"Hey!" Graham is overcompensating, like awkwardness can be covered by enthusiasm.

I hear Jonathan say something. It's a mumble, and I can't even guess what he said.

"What?" I walk over to him.

I'm standing there stupidly in front of Jonathan, waiting for him to repeat whatever it was he said.

Jonathan sighs, stepping down. He puts his hand on my shoulder. "You look like a trip," he says. "That's a compliment, baby sister."

But I still can't make myself smile for him.

"What did you *really* say?" My brother doesn't whisper compliments, he spews them proudly because he knows what a gift they are coming from him—what they used to be to everyone, and still are to me.

"I said, 'Have fun.' That's all." He nods at Graham and raises his voice. "Have fun."

"Sure—will do," Graham says, turning red and smiling back nervously.

It's all wrong, and I wonder if Graham can sense it, too. A boy taking me out—*all night*, to be exact—wouldn't have gotten away without a few threats from my older brother.

Jonathan stands there silently, leaning against the banister at the bottom of the stairs, watching as Standard Dad continues to take pictures and Mumsy instructs me on how to stand. I watch him right back. The forlornness seems to start at his toes, hitting his knees, then his hips, then his shoulders, finally presenting itself on his face. I wonder if he's thinking about Grace. How at least he was able to give her the ultimate Garfield High experience, invites to the best parties, front-row seats at the football games, before he took away all the rest.

"Amanda, smile," Mumsy says. And I do, because this is supposed to be a happy occasion, and I don't want to ruin it.

CHAPTER
SEVEN

Lights flashing, loud music, streamers. Stars everywhere, hanging from the ceiling, lining the walls, stuck to the backs of the chairs, taking the theme of Magic Under the Stars very seriously.

I spend the beginning of the dance in the foyer of the hotel's ballroom, rambling away about whatever pops into my head to Dawn's voice mail until it cuts me off. I debate going outside, taking a walk, but it's raining. I'm killing time. I planned this brief absence from the dance so that people have the chance to ask Graham if he saw Jonathan, as I know they're bound to do. This way they can get it out of their systems, while I'm not there. *Jonathan Tart, thin as a rail. Jonathan Tart, barely conscious, maybe drunk. Jonathan Tart, not nearly as cheeky as he was on* Lifeline.

I hope they talk. Even if it's about how awful he seems to be doing. Even if they think he deserves it. I don't want my brother to be the boy who killed Grace and sulks up in his room, but I don't want him to be the boy on *Lifeline* either. I hope they cancel each other out, make way for the new boy my brother will become. He'll have grief that doesn't rot him, remorse that doesn't suck the life out of him. He'll laugh again, but never about things he can't take back. He'll find his place in the world, and he won't be so wild.

And he won't contact Sutton Crane, unless it's to tell her he's sorry.

"Too bad it's too cloudy outside to see the stars tonight. The theme should really be Magic Under the Clouds," Graham points out when I rejoin him in the ballroom. It feels good to laugh. Even dancing is fun tonight.

A song dedication goes out to the seniors, and they all shuffle onto the dance floor. It's an outpouring of sweaty hugs, a chorus of *I'll miss you*, and tears—of course, already—because even though there are still months and months to spend together before the end of the year, everyone already knows how the loss is going to weigh on them.

I will remember you. . . .

It's bittersweet for them, even I can tell. Though I'm not really a part of it until Graham tucks an arm around me and holds me close to him. He takes me with him as he gives one-armed hugs to his teammates and squeezes the hands of girls he's served with on the student council all these years.

Henry is a few feet away. Easy to spot, as he always is for me, and he's in the dead center of the dance floor, bending forward, making out with his girlfriend, Imogen West. Very classy. Probably also very distracting. He doesn't have to think about saying good-bye, or the person we never got the chance to say it to, if he's completely consumed with Imogen. I think about occupying myself in the same way. But Graham's deep in conversation with someone else.

"I know it's not as sad for you, because Dawn has already left," Graham says, to explain to himself the reason my mascara is still intact.

I can't cry. I'm not allowed. Even here. He doesn't understand.

"It's still sad," I offer. But he doesn't hear me. I have to tug on his arm until he looks at me. "I'm going to miss you."

His mouth turns down, and right away I know it was the wrong thing to say. We don't talk about next year, after we graduate, when I'll hopefully be in Santa Barbara and all his plans leave him in Chicago. I worry that declaring that we won't be together next year before either of us has even gotten our college acceptances is the equivalent of a *Lifeline* breakup. I'm holding on to his arm so tightly my knuckles feel like they're going to pop off.

"We can—we'll figure it out," I say, pulling myself close to him. "Right?"

He melts into my arms, but not before giving me a smile so full of heart that I really do want to cry a little, just for him. I pull him close and shut my eyes so I can't see Henry. It's such a relief, for once, to have the right lines.

CHAPTER
EIGHT

Limos drop us off at the after-homecoming party at a rented house twenty miles north and remain "on call" the rest of the night. The drivers give us handfuls of their cards. *Ride free tonight!* is written in purple block letters above the phone number. This arrangement was organized by the school and parents—they raised donations to cover the cost of renting all the limos for the night. Most parents were probably very generous. I know mine were. And it's great publicity for the limo companies, thanks to an article that made the Saturday edition of the *Chicago Tribune*.

The ride was full of *shh, be quiet*, as everyone got on the phone with their parents to check in, which in most cases involved reinforcing the lie they'd told. *I'm sleeping over at Lacey's, that's right.* My parents never required lies, as they never set curfews. I heard my mother say once, "At least he wasn't on his way home," about Jonathan on the night of the accident. Her absolution, twisted into a nod to her no-curfew policy. They know I'm not coming home tonight, and they didn't ask for details.

We pull up to a monstrosity of a house with a wraparound porch and big windows, at the end of a long driveway, with tall, thick trees surrounding it. It's the kind of house that looks like it should be backed up against a lake.

"There are, like, a million bedrooms," one of Graham's soccer buddies informs us.

Graham blushes.

I smile at them, nodding, so they'll know I understand the excitement. Really I'm praying that whatever room we end up in, it's far away from Henry and Imogen. Tonight marks another failed attempt at keeping Henry off my radar.

After just twenty minutes of exploring the giant house, we all end up in the kitchen. There's enough pizza to feed an army, and an entire refrigerator full of soda. There's a lot of beer, too, purchased at a mini-mart fifteen miles away that is known to never card. Someone's older sister hooked the party up with vodka. It's in a bottle that's three times the size of a regular bottle and made of plastic. If my brother has taught me anything, it's that you don't drink the liquor that comes in plastic bottles. He gave me this advice while resting his head on the toilet in the upstairs bathroom. It's not to be taken lightly.

Graham tries to score me a wine cooler, but they're gone in a flash, downed by the girls' soccer team, if their dark-red lips serve as a tell.

There's a Ping-Pong table in the basement. I get a few games in with Graham before it's turned into a beer-pong table. Though it's his first time playing beer pong, Graham is actually very skilled, and people fight to be his partner. He's got a spot at the table all night, as he remains undefeated. Everyone is bouncing off the walls—so many people to talk to, so much to talk about. I can't keep up. I shut myself in the room with my stuff, and no one comes after me. It's sort of a relief. I'm a little afraid that people, drunk, with all inhibitions off duty, might have things to say about my brother.

The room Graham and I chose is at the very end of the hall on the lower level. It's far away from the family room, and from the bathroom—which sounds inconvenient, but will actually help us sleep better, since we won't be woken up every time someone has to vomit in the middle of the night. It's a small, narrow afterthought sort of room, with round windows, wood paneling, and an exposed lightbulb on the ceiling. There are denim duvets and red throw pillows on the matching twin beds. I joked with Graham that we'd be like Lucy and Ricky Ricardo. He didn't hear me. He was too busy pushing the beds together.

I changed out of my dress and into yoga pants and a T-shirt earlier, like all the other girls did. By now my curls are heavy and crunchy, and my scalp is itchy. I examine myself in the dingy mirror, which has *Newcastle* written across it. My makeup has molded to my skin, and there are dark specks around my eyes that blur, but don't wipe away, when I rub them.

"Hey, pretty girl." Graham leans against the doorway. He can manage to stay balanced for only a second before he slides into the door.

Jonathan's voice pops into my head. "I can't believe you're dating such a lightweight," he would say if he were here.

"Hey there." I move to help prop him up, but he straightens before I reach him.

Graham is drunk, which was probably an accident, something that snuck up on him while he was busy being beer-pong champion, but I know he's okay with it, because tonight he can be blitzed out of his mind while still being responsible. We have a limo driver if we want to leave. A room to sleep in if we want to stay. I should probably be drunk, too. I mean, what an opportunity.

His eyelids dip, and he laughs. I help him onto the bed and sit next to him, so we're leaning against the wall with our feet out in front of us.

"You looked so beautiful tonight." He hiccups. "Still do."

"You're not so bad yourself." I kiss him on his adorable and perfectly clean-shaven cheek.

He sighs and lets his head hang. It jerks itself upright when he hiccups again. "I can't believe that was our last homecoming."

"I know." I play along. If he wasn't drunk, I'd have to try harder to make my enthusiasm believable. "At least we all had the chance to say good-bye," I say, referencing the senior dedication at the dance.

"You're really depressing sometimes," he says. His eyes blink back tears, and he jerks away from me.

He's right.

"I'm sorry." I have to dig my fingers into his shirt; he's so intent on ignoring me. "I'm really messed up, you know that. I'm just—"

"I know that," he says louder, slurring, but at least looking at me now. "I know that most of all. But it's for nothing. Okay? Believe it, because it's the factual truth. Jonathan was like, fuck off, I go where I wanna go and you can come or you can stay behind. And everyone always wanted to come." He hiccups. "Everyone always came."

"Okay," I say. "You're right."

He nods, triumphant, but he's too close to passing out to enjoy his victory.

"I'm sorry I messed this up for us," he tells me as I pull off his shoes and drape the comforter over him.

"I probably would have 'had a headache' anyway." I wait for him to laugh, but he's already asleep.

"Good night," I whisper. I hope he forgets this conversation.

CHAPTER NINE

I stand up to close the door so we can go to sleep, but there's a pair of eyes staring back at me from the hallway. Henry leans against the wall. I don't have to study him long to know he, too, is drunk. More than anything else, he seems forlorn. What a party this has turned out to be. He looks at me and his face is all shadows, except for a smirk.

I move into the hallway and close the door softly behind me.

"What, Henry?" I ask, getting defensive. There's something so off-putting about the way he's got his arms crossed, the way his eyes are playing sinister, the way he's smiling. It's not his usual demeanor, or his usual smile.

"Sometimes Imogen calls me depressing, too." He shrugs. "I

didn't mean to eavesdrop, but the door was open." He covers his mouth with his hand. It seems like he's about to crack up. This hurts my feelings and makes me angrier than I've been in a long time.

"Go back to the party—" I turn and reach for the doorknob.

"I have to talk to you," he says, his voice getting louder.

I'm slow to face him, not sure I want to hear it.

Now that I'm looking at him, he stares at my feet. "I'm here to confrontation—to confront . . . I have a bone to pick with you. . . ." He licks his lips, and now his smile says that he's embarrassed. "It's not good."

"What could be worse than you stalking me at a party and lurking outside my room?"

He lets out a shallow laugh. "I actually followed Graham."

"Still sketchy."

"We have an important matter to discuss. It'd be nice if you'd take it seriously."

"Well, Henry, then it's a good thing you've chosen right now, when you need the wall to hold yourself up, to approach me about this very serious and important issue."

He shakes his head, laughing lightly like I'm the one who's had too much to drink and isn't making any sense. To his credit, he lifts himself off the wall and doesn't fall over. "I know that they're talking, Amanda. I *know*. You were supposed to tell me."

"I had no idea they were talking." *I had no idea Sutton was here*, I once told an angry Henry, who showed up at my front door at midnight looking for his sister after she'd missed a dinner with their grandmother and failed to return his many messages. This time he doesn't believe me.

"Okay, sure."

"Why would I—" But I stop myself. His eyes have that faraway haze to them, and he's got that drunken confidence, complete with tunnel vision and selective hearing that makes people doubly confrontational and blind in their determination. "We can talk about this tomorrow."

"No, no, we can't." He steps forward so he's got one hand on the door and his back to the hall—his half-baked attempt at blocking me in.

"How do you even know it was Jonathan she was speaking to?"

"She had this . . ." Every ounce of resolve deflates from Henry's expression. "This look on her face."

I know exactly what he's talking about. Sutton with Jonathan was Sutton unmasked. She turned giddy and indulgent, and her face revealed how she marveled at my brother. Like the cat that swallowed the canary. Normally, Sutton wore a scowl better than anyone, except she couldn't muster one for the life of her if Jonathan was around. Her usual expression—cranky, intimidating, unpredictable, like she might bite your head off if you said the wrong thing or looked at her the wrong way, and she had the reputation to back these assumptions—cracked and softened. Sometimes, next to him, she looked like she was holding in too much happiness for one person. I thought that maybe explained the motive behind her evil eye—she had a lot to lose.

"You're wrong," I say, even though it's pointless to get into it with him when he's like this. "Jonathan told me he wasn't participating in telecommunications."

Henry shoots me a glare, like he can tell I've use Jonathan's exact words again.

"They're lying to us, to everyone," he says. "Just like the good old days."

Except in the good old days there was at least Grace keeping them honest, calling them out on their lies. Henry pinches his eyes closed, as though it takes a great effort. The hallway is probably spinning. Or he's thinking about Grace, too.

Maybe Jonathan did lie to me. Maybe he talked to Sutton. Maybe he told her everything he should have said before he left. Maybe he's the only one who can understand how much she misses Grace, and their twisted relationship can survive this grief just like it's managed to endure everything else: Sutton's temper, Jonathan's wandering eye. Has Henry ever considered that it might be okay—good, even—for them to talk?

"I guess, if they are talking, who are we to stop them?"

"You don't understand," he says, raking his hands through his hair.

"It might not be the worst thing in the world, you know?" I let my tone counter his. Optimism all around. Drunk people are quick to turn angry, but quick to buy into idealism, too. "It might help both of them—"

"He ruined her!" His voice vibrates off the walls.

"Henry, be quiet—"

"When she was in the hospital, he didn't come to see her once; he didn't even call when she got out—" He breaks off, his eyes getting glassier by the second. "If that would've been you, I would have never left your side. They would've had to drag me away."

He's got to be wasted to be talking like this, and now that I really look at him, his eyes aren't filling with tears of sadness or even anger. This is just what he looks like when he's plastered. The eyes are always the first to go. I remind myself that he's out of his mind. It means nothing that he put me in the car with him instead of Imogen.

"He didn't even go to her funeral," Henry says. "Even though he used to claim he loved Grace as much as he loved his baby sister."

He gives me a second to let this sink in. I want to push Henry for comparing Grace to me, like it's the only way I could possibly comprehend how much she meant to Jonathan.

It takes some time before I can find my voice. I don't even really think about what I'm saying. "You know it was impossible for him to be at the funeral when he was—?"

"When he was the reason there was a funeral in the first place?"

Not what I was going to say at all, but Henry's face glows victorious, before it darkens again. The lawyers told Jonathan to stay out of the public eye, to mourn in private with his friends and family. Even if he'd wanted to go, he wasn't allowed. Henry has no idea. And if he doesn't understand this, then maybe he's not giving Jonathan enough credit regarding Sutton either.

"Maybe Jonathan's apologized to her," I say.

I'm cut off by Henry's cruel laughter.

"I don't know why I thought I could talk to you about this!" he shouts. "You're in such serious denial about who your brother is. And even more clueless about how destructive he is to other people." He moves toward me, until he's close enough that I can smell his faded cologne and the beer on his breath. "Well over a year later, and even with a healthy dose of antidepressants in her system, Sutton's still barely hanging on. He's the poison that could push her over the edge."

Or maybe Jonathan's the only one who could pull Sutton back, I want to tell him. But even I can see the hopelessness in expecting anything from Jonathan; and the stupidity in thinking he's a person who can save anyone.

"We don't have a deal anymore, do we?" Henry says.

I shake my head. Right now all I can think about is this one day in the hall when I was walking behind Jonathan, Sutton, and Grace on my way to class. Jonathan was between them, one hand entwined with Sutton's, the other on Grace's shoulder.

"Grace would have wanted them to talk," I say.

"Everything Grace would have wanted is wrecked because of him."

I cover my eyes with my hands, trying to pull myself back together. I'm sure there are tears gathering under my eyes, but I let my hands fall anyway. Henry's moved closer to me. His breathing has picked up. His eyes are so watery, there's no doubt in my mind that sadness has beat out both anger and inebriation. Even if my experience with drunk boys is rusty now thanks to Jonathan's absence, my intuition tells me that Henry's about to fall apart, and he's going to do it in my arms.

Behind him, I see shadows. No—people, crowding around the far end of the hallway, listening to us. I don't know how long they've been there, or how much they've heard, and I try to remember if I saw them when the shouting first started. The door next to me opens and Graham steps out, with one eye open, his hair sticking straight up.

I knew we were being loud but had no idea we were loud enough to attract an audience.

Graham runs a hand over his face. I'm not sure he knows he's awake.

"It's okay. Go back to bed," I say, moving to help him and planning to disappear into the room with him. But Graham's attention has turned to the girl pushing her way through the crowd. Imogen West. Henry's girlfriend since the Fourth of July.

"Henry?" Imogen staggers down the hall toward us. She's got a hand on her hip, and her eyes are wide and angry, ready for a fight. She notices me and her expression hardens. She switches from defense to offense. I would cash in all my chips betting Henry never told her about our twenty-four-hour relationship. I'm Jonathan Tart's little sister, and that is enough. She stiffens and reaches for Henry's hand.

"Come on—"

He jerks away from her, but he cringes like he's immediately sorry he did.

"Come on, Henry." She moves closer to him. "Don't be like this," she whispers, but I'm close enough to hear the pleading in her voice. "Not on the night of our last homecoming. Please." This time when she reaches for his hand, he lets her take it. She leads him down the hall and through the slowly dispersing group at the end of the hallway. He follows without looking back.

Texting with Dawn, Monday, 12:47 p.m.

Answer your phone?

Hungover. Can't handle noise.

Not even the sweet, sweet melody of my lovely voice? ☺

Too much boxed wine in the common room last night. Oops. But it was a Freaks and Geeks drinking game, so I'm not sorry.

What was the game?

We drank anytime someone acted like a freak or a geek.

Wow, you college kids are so clever.

Hey, we study so hard, our brains deserve a vacation.

Today is the worst.

It's Monday, duh. What's wrong? ☹

People won't look at me.

Good. People can keep their eyes to themselves for once.

They're saying I screamed at Henry at the after-homecoming party because Henry said Jonathan deserved to be in jail. That's not how it went down at all.

But didn't you scream at him a little?

The real story is the one I told you yesterday. I raised my voice at him only AFTER he raised his voice at me. And I didn't mean to defend Jonathan, but Henry really hates him. He thinks he's going to ruin Sutton's life, even though they aren't even talking. He's the one who got drunk and decided to take his hatred of Jonathan out on me. But now I'm the one who's like a pariah.

You've always been like a pariah. ☺

Haha.

You should tell the real story of what happened. Submit it to the school paper! That will show them!

Was that a Freaks and Geeks plotline or something?

As if I can remember things like plotlines after last night. My skull hurts.

Poor Dawn.

Remember you only have 141 days left.

Lunch is almost over. I've got to go. Miss you.

Miss you back.

CHAPTER TEN

*G*raham meets me by my locker. We've still got a few more minutes before the bell rings and dismisses us from lunch. I can tell by the way he hesitates before he greets me that something is on his mind.

"Yes?" I nudge him.

"I was just thinking . . . you never told me what happened, you know—why you were yelling at Henry on Saturday night." He's put on a voice that's careful and padded. *Let's not wake the beast.*

"He was yelling at me, too." My voice sounds defensive, and I instantly feel bad. Graham glances to the hall, at all the people who've turned their backs on me, and scratches his forehead with his thumb. This is Graham's tell: he feels uncomfortable. It's not his fault; I'm sure he had no idea when he woke up today that his girlfriend would stand accused of defending Jonathan Tart while screaming at Henry, whose poor sister is still suffering. "Henry was totally smashed and, I don't know, it was like the only way he'd hear me was for me to yell back." I don't add that I hardly remember yelling at all, because Graham trusts whatever his friends have told him.

"What'd he say to you?" Graham asks.

I shake my head, giving a slight shrug. A shiver runs up my spine. *If that would've been you, I would have never left your side.* "He was just upset because he thought Jonathan was trying to reach Sutton. I tried to tell him that Jonathan wasn't in touch with anyone. He wouldn't listen."

Graham does not like this one bit. His eyebrows dip.

"It's fine," I tell him, reaching out my hand because I know he'll take it. "Like I said, he was drunk."

Graham nods. He squeezes my hand. This excuse gets people off the hook for anything. *Almost* anything.

Later, I walk into sixth period early and sit in my seat by the window. Henry arrives early, too. He takes a seat in the middle this time, right next to mine.

CHAPTER ELEVEN

Henry doesn't say anything, doesn't even look at me, as the room fills up. Bryan walks awkwardly up to his usual desk, now occupied by Henry. He lets out a quick laugh, and I expect it to be followed by "Hey, man, you're in my seat." But his eyes shift to me, and then he moves to the opposite side of the room.

I try my best to listen as Mr. Scott details our next assignment. He caps off his explanation with the dreaded words, "Partner up."

This is where I pretend to be looking for something in the textbook, flipping the pages back and forth, like I'm much, much too busy to worry about being anyone's partner—and

definitely too occupied to notice how no one is looking my way, wanting to pair up.

A pen taps against my desk, three sharp knocks. It's Henry. He's turned sideways in his chair and is reaching across the aisle to get my attention.

He raises his eyebrows in an almost friendly manner. "What do you say, Amanda?"

Amander.

I feel my mouth drop open, but I keep my eyes on him, too scared to look at anyone else in the room—they all probably look as shocked as I do.

Henry smiles—he actually smiles.

He begins sliding his desk closer to mine, the way the rest of the class has positioned themselves. But I'm still too mystified to move.

"Don't make me do all the work," he says, reaching forward and tugging on the legs of my desk, closing the gap. But his voice—it's light and playful.

I cut to the chase. "Why are you doing this?"

"Convenience," he says. This joke doesn't take, so he tries another. "You know I'm not a bloody picky lad when it comes to partners." He looks at me expectantly.

In our past life, I wouldn't have let this go. *Lad? Bloody?* No, Henry is not British enough to say *bloody* or *lad*. This is him playing up Britishisms to annoy me the way he did when he first moved here.

Now I just look at him, straight-faced and somber, and he finally caves.

"Because." He clears his throat and lowers his voice. "Who else was going to be your partner?"

"Well, I . . ." I want to point out Ellen Lapin, who serves on the student council with Graham and probably would have been my partner out of pity, or as a favor to Graham. But now that I've been caught in the hallway at the homecoming after-party, defending Jonathan Tart, I wouldn't expect her to offer.

"And," Henry says quietly, his eyes suddenly looking down. I can see the apology before I hear it. "I'm sorry I cornered you outside your room and yelled at you . . . it was misdirected anger, and I was off my face, and . . . I'm sorry."

"You were a real wanker."

"I was. And I'm so sorry."

"So this"—I tick my finger back and forth to indicate the two of us—"this is a peace offering?"

He nods once, then opens his hands, palms up, and shrugs. "I know it's not much."

"Okay," I say, trying my best not to sound skeptical. This could work. We'll just have topics that are off-limits. He can go on hating Jonathan, and it doesn't have to affect this project. And maybe it will actually help. Maybe people will forget there are reasons they don't want to look at me, since Henry—*the victim*, according to the rumors—has forgiven me enough to be my partner. Perhaps someone was eavesdropping and caught his apology. No matter how quietly he said it. "I'm sorry, too. For yelling back and . . . everything." *Everything.* For not knowing how to talk to him about the things that matter, about the grief that we share, instead of the hatred we don't. *I'm sorry.*

"Oh, come on. You know that's not necessary. Half the time when I yell at you, I'm only doing it so you'll yell back."

That's not allowed, I think. Smiling, and talking to me all casually, like we haven't just come off of a sixteen-month-long hiatus.

Mr. Scott claps to get our attention and continues class. I follow along and pretend my life is typical.

CHAPTER
TWELVE

"What are you doing home?" My mother greets me in the entryway when I get home from school, wearing heels and a gray dress. Her hair is curled and pinned back, and her makeup is done.

"Open seventh," I remind her, since usually at this time she's in her room, presumably napping—a habit she developed after Jonathan's arrest, when the days suddenly became too long for her. I set my backpack under the side table, and she picks it up.

"Upstairs," she demands, thrusting it at me.

The doorbell rings, and Jonathan rushes past me down the stairs. He's in a light-blue button-down, khakis, and brown dress shoes. And his clothes fit.

Mumsy pats the back of her hair, straightens the bottom of her skirt. When she opens the door, she greets the person on the other side with her friendliest smile.

"You must be Gary. Please, come in." She even sounds cheerful. "I'm Angela, Jonathan's mother."

Jonathan stalls at the bottom of the stairs but eventually steps forward and shakes hands with the man standing in the foyer, murmuring, "Nice to see you again." He's a younger guy—midtwenties maybe, though his red hair is already thinning on top. I don't know what else to do when he looks up at me standing there, staring, so I give him an awkward wave. He waves back.

"Oh," my mother says, letting out a high, bubbly laugh. "That's my daughter, Amanda. She's a senior with a lot of free periods, so that's why she's home so early from school."

The man extends his hand to me. There are an awkward couple of seconds as I walk down to meet him, then have to move my backpack to my left hand so my right hand is free to shake his.

"Gary," he says. My handshake isn't nearly as sturdy as his. "You're his sister? It'd be good for you to join us, then."

"Okay." I glance to Mumsy, and she gives me a nod as though she supports this idea. The tight lines of her smile suggest otherwise.

I follow behind them into the living room and take a seat on the couch next to Jonathan. Gary and my mother sit across from us in wingback chairs. Gary crosses his legs and pulls a clipboard out of his messenger bag.

"This is Jonathan's probation officer," Mumsy says to me, her voice turning pleasant.

"Let's get started, shall we?" Gary flips to the third page on his clipboard. He scratches the place on his head that will probably go bald first as he explains the terms of Jonathan's probation, reading directly off the paper, not once looking up.

"There's one matter we should get out of the way right now." Gary reaches into his messenger bag. He pulls out a plastic cup with a red lid and sets it on the coffee table in front of Jonathan.

"Urine, semen, or blood?" Of all the times for Jonathan to start making jokes again—what is he thinking? I close my eyes, wishing it wasn't totally inappropriate for me to elbow Jonathan in the ribs.

Gary starts to say "Urine," but notes that Jonathan is smirking, and gives a close-lipped smile. "For the EtG test, to test for ethanol . . . to determine if alcohol is present in your . . ." He watches as Jonathan leaves, looking concerned, like maybe he's not completely convinced that Jonathan's going to bring back what he's supposed to.

We all sit there, my mother locking her hand around her crossed legs and giving us a smile that's nowhere near genuine, Gary fumbling with his clipboard pages. I find myself nodding to the quiet.

"Have you been doing this long?" is the question my mother chooses to break the silence.

"No, ma'am." He looks up for a beat before hunching farther over his clipboard.

"How long?" she asks.

"Actually," he says, straightening up, "now would be a good time for you to share your transportation plan."

"Our transportation plan—oh, you mean since Jonathan can't—his license is . . . Yes, yes, of course. I'm free to drive him during the day, and both his father and I are available in the evenings."

I raise my hand. "And I can take him on the weekends." I stifle a giggle, wishing Jonathan were here, since he would probably find this comment, paired with my raised hand, as silly as I do.

"There's no reason Jonathan shouldn't travel independently." Gary pulls transit schedules from his bag and sets them on the coffee table.

"Of course." My mother looks out the window. I catch her doing one of her yoga breaths, deep in, slowly out.

Jonathan comes back, and I have never been so happy to see him, even standing there holding his own urine.

Gary hands Jonathan packets of paper and several pamphlets and proceeds to ask a lot of questions about things like Jonathan's daily routine and what he likes to do in his free time. Jonathan's answers consist of a variety of *I don't know*s and *haven't thought about it*s.

"Will you be enforcing a curfew?" Gary asks my mother.

She smiles, stalling, and finally settles on, "Ten p.m."

Gary writes this down, and my mother inspects his expressionless face for signs that she's answered correctly.

"Please list the names of friends you'll be keeping in touch with regularly." Gary turns to Jonathan, his legs crossed to balance the clipboard and his hand ready to write.

"No one," Jonathan says without hesitation.

Gary stares frozen with his pen hovering over the clipboard, like he's waiting for more—a punch line, probably—before he scribbles down the answer.

He clears his throat and proceeds, asking about Jonathan's plans for community service.

"Can't I just pick up garbage off the side of the road like the rest of the delinquents?" is Jonathan's charming response.

Mumsy is quick in her attempt to distract from this one. "What did you have in mind, Gary?"

"Well—" He flips back a page or two. "A nonprofit called Chicago Cares was hoping you would speak about your experience this last year, about your incarceration . . . and about the incident that landed you in prison. They'll be dropping in on local high schools. They'd like for you to join them. Share your story."

Jonathan back at Garfield High. The thought of it makes my heart race. My mother's hands are choking each other.

Jonathan squints. "Are you kidding?"

Gary looks at his notebook again, shaking his head. "No, I think—"

"I've already shared my story," Jonathan says, leaning forward. "With *everyone*."

"The organization is more than aware of . . . your past with public speaking."

This description makes Mumsy's eyebrows twitch against the Botox.

"Listen," Gary says, more to his clipboard than to anyone else, "this is a great opportunity for community service, as required by your probation, with a reputable organization that has been a strong supporter of drunk-driving awareness campaigns. I would recommend taking advantage of it."

Jonathan leans back, crosses his arms. There's no way he'll agree to this, I think—I hope.

After a few seconds of quiet, Gary continues, reading again from what's in front of him. "Have you given any thought to your future plans? There's a note here that you might reenroll in—"

"We'll take all your suggestions under advisement," Jonathan interrupts.

My mother perks up, noting she's part of what Jonathan meant by *we'll*. I've seen Jonathan do this before—group people with him, create sides. His side always won, so most of the time, it was a good thing to be recruited by Jonathan. Graduation night, he'd done it. *We've got places to go, people to see, champagne to pop.* An arm around Sutton. A wink fired at Grace.

"I need to know how you'll be structuring your days out of federal custody," Gary says.

"We're still considering options," Mumsy says. "He hasn't even been home a week."

Gary nods at Jonathan. "Lots to think about. You'll let me know next time. This meeting was a home visit, but next time it'll be at my office. Do you need the address—"

"I know where to find you," Jonathan says, waving one of the packets Gary gave him during the meeting.

Mumsy takes this cue and stands, so Jonathan and I do, too. I feel bad when Gary notices how ready we are for him to leave and rushes to put his coat on, tucking the clipboard under his arm instead of bothering to fit it back in his bag. He almost forgets Jonathan's urine on the coffee table and has to double back to get it. He probably has a special ice chest, minus the ice, filled with urine sitting on the floor of his car. He probably has to stare into the eyes of several hardened criminals every day, ask them for their pee, and spend the remaining twenty minutes nagging them with advice on how to *not* wind up back in prison. Hopefully some of them see him for the advocate he's trying to be—the way Jonathan should have.

"One more thing," Gary says. My mother's holding the door open for him, and he's just two steps from the doormat. "Here." He sets down his messenger bag so he has a free hand, then fishes around in the side pocket of his messenger bag and presents Jonathan with a pamphlet. "I recommend going as a sort of therapy, a way to keep yourself in check. Even when you're feeling good and in control, it can help."

Jonathan makes no effort to take the pamphlet from him, so Gary sets it on the edge of the side table, where it teeters and falls.

I catch it. It's a brochure for Alcoholics Anonymous, listing all the meetings in the area.

"Thank you." It comes out of me like a reflex. It's a relief when Gary smiles.

Mumsy flaps her hand up and down at him quickly. It's less of a farewell and more like she's rushing him out. Before getting in his car, he looks back at us once more—the waving family with the icy eyes.

"I'll see what we can do about getting you someone else," my mother says, patting Jonathan on the shoulder as she passes him on her way to the kitchen.

"Thanks," he tells her.

"Does it really matter?" I ask. "Aren't they all the same?"

"One who doesn't have stupid ideas about community service and actually cares about what I'm going to have to deal with the next ten years would be nice." He's already unbuttoning his dress shirt, already headed up the stairs to shut himself away.

"You know, it's easier to care about you when you're not an asshole," I call to his back.

I hear the door to his room shut. I'm about to rush up the stairs after him, try for some answers as to why he was such a dick to his probation officer, but I see my mother leaning against the counter, looking at me incredulously. The same way she was looking at Gary.

CHAPTER
THIRTEEN

On Tuesday Graham claims he has radar for when I'm upset. But really, the hallway gossip has told him.

"Maybe you can switch partners?" he says, giving my hand an extra squeeze.

"It's for one assignment," I say. "I'll live."

The rumors have said otherwise: Henry and I were forced to be partners, even though we both asked the teacher to change who we were paired with. Henry's my partner to gain intel about Jonathan, like a spy whose sole mission is sending Jonathan back to jail. Some are closer to the truth: Henry's only my partner because he feels bad for yelling at me at the homecoming after-party. Either way, Graham is very concerned.

He pulls me in for a hug, and I make sure to count to five in my head before I let go. I kiss him fast on the lips, the only way we'll ever be caught kissing in public, because we're both embarrassed by PDA, and head off to my sixth-period class to face Henry.

Or ignore him. Which is what I plan to do. In fact, I've spent the entire day convincing myself Henry and I can do this entire measly assignment of interviewing a local business owner without really interacting with each other. We'll show up at Ludwig's Doughnuts—the business we've been assigned—and sit side by side wearing smiles, one of us asking the questions while the other takes down the answers.

I've got the laptop in front of me. Just a quick finalization of the interview questions and I'll be ready to go.

But Henry taps his pen next to my finger on the keyboard; this was always the most annoying way he invaded my personal space to get my attention.

"It's kind of funny," he says.

I don't take my eyes off the computer, and I continue to type. Henry should be happy that I've taken the administrative part of the project under my wing. He could spend this time catching up on homework or playing solitaire or napping, for all I care. "I doubt that, but go ahead and tell me anyway."

"We both hate doughnuts."

It's true. We prefer savory breakfast food, a fact we learned the night we thought we'd be waking up to have breakfast together.

I try to pretend he doesn't faze me and keep my fingers moving, but the letters popping up on the screen do not form words.

"You spelled 'doughnut' wrong," Henry says, looking over my shoulder. "There's no *p*."

Carefully, I remove my hands from the keyboard. "I could use a break," I say, sliding the laptop onto his desk. "You take over."

"Amanda—"

With a quick glance to the clock, I realize that Dawn has just gotten out of class. I slide my cell into my back pocket, get up from my desk, snatch the pass from the front of the room, and power walk down the hall.

I'm a few yards from the bathroom when I hear my name. *Amander.*

Henry jogs to catch up with me.

"Hey, where are you going?" he says, stepping in front of me.

I nod in the direction of the restroom. "There was no need to chase after me."

"Mr. Scott thought I'd upset you and sent me to apologize."

"That's ridiculous."

"Well, you did leave in a bit of a huff."

"I did not."

"Look," he says, "to me it's perfectly clear there's nothing wrong and that I did nothing to 'upset' you. But Mr. Scott thinks you're distressed and that it's because of me, so will you please come back to class and straighten this out?"

"That's so unnecessary—"

"Was it the mere mention of doughnuts that troubled you?"

"Henry."

"I mean, I know you prefer your morning sugar intake via lattes, but I'm sure the owner of Ludwig's won't be offended when neither of us orders—"

"I'm not upset!"

He eyes me. "Of course not."

"I didn't leave in a huff; I just *left*. People have to stop pinning anger on me." There's no way to shake him off. I just want to be standing in the bathroom listening to Dawn rant about bio, imagining what it'll be like when I'm there with her and far, far away from here, and all this.

"In Mr. Scott's defense, remember eighth grade, language arts. . . ."

That's right. Before Mr. Scott started teaching sophomore English and senior Consumer Economics, he was at Millbrook Middle School. I remember the fight, clear as day. Henry stole the poem I'd written for class—he'd ripped one of my earlier drafts from my notebook when I wasn't looking, and as soon as Mr. Scott asked for volunteers to share theirs, Henry raised his hand. I turned seven shades of pink as Henry read my poor attempt at rhyming in an ode to Miguel Lowery—the boy that everyone had a crush on in eighth grade—to the entire class. If the class had known it was my poem, making the Miguel connection would have been easy, as not many other eighth-grade boys were tall enough to "reach the stars" or had hair that was both "as long as the Mississippi River" and "the color of ravens." But no one laughed. Go figure, my lame poem spun with a British accent actually sounded profound.

"It's about being homesick," someone guessed.

"It's about being left behind."

"It's about his dead grandfather."

Grace was in the class too. "It's a love poem about a dude," she said, and grinned with delight, given how much of a fuss all the *girls* in our class made over Henry.

I walked up to Mr. Scott's desk first thing when class was over, in what I suppose some might call a huff, and demanded that Henry apologize to me in front of the whole class for taking credit for my poem. It turned out that the only thing worse than everyone finding out about my crush on Miguel was Henry taking the credit for a poem everyone actually liked.

The next day Henry said he was sorry, admitted to his crime, and read aloud his own poem, which was without a doubt about soccer and nothing deeper. Grace was visibly disappointed by this revelation.

It's all storm clouds between us in the hallway now, with thunder too loud to talk over. Because we both remember Grace sitting there with her arms crossed over her desk, her shoulders rolling forward as she sighed, listening to Henry's confession. "We can go back," I say, and my voice breaks a bit.

"I'll go," Henry says. "I'll tell him you're fine, it's all cleared up, and that you'll be returning soon."

"It's okay. I only left to call Dawn. I can do it later."

We walk back to class slowly. He stays to the right side of the hall and I stay to the left.

TEXT MESSAGE TO DAWN, NEVER SENT, TUESDAY, 8:30 P.M.

She was there, and now she's not. She played tetherball at recess; I played tag. But she was there. She was on the volleyball team; I ran track. We were both in choir; she sang alto, I was a soprano. She was at ragers on Saturday nights. I was with you, most likely at the movies. But around seven at night, when we were getting ready to leave the house, stocking up on candy from the stash Mumsy thought was a secret, and Jonathan and Sutton were rounding up Jose, Jim, and Jack, she was there.

CHAPTER
FOURTEEN

Jonathan is standing in the kitchen, soaked in sweat and chugging water, when I come downstairs at six thirty a.m. on Wednesday morning. This is usually the time I'm getting ready to roll out of bed. It's so early, I'm surprised to find Jonathan awake, let alone standing in the kitchen with Standard Dad, who's leaning against the counter, buttering his toast, getting ready to leave for work.

"What happened to you?" I ask Jonathan. Detoxing, is what I'd guess, if these were the old days. But he's got a sparkle in his eyes, and the edges of his mouth aren't pointing down like they normally are when he's getting the booze out of his system. Endorphins are most likely to blame.

He's still breathing too heavily to speak.

"He ran to Starbucks and back," my dad says. He grabs his thermos out of the cabinet and pats Jonathan on the back as he passes.

"Why Starbucks?" I squint at Jonathan, so he'll know I've got him figured out. Whenever Jonathan does something new or different, the motivation is typically female, and in this case she comes in the form of a barista with a mouth like a sailor and a smoking habit she uses for flirting, who couldn't play it cool enough to keep from gushing over my brother's eyes. He was never one to *go for a run* before. It's not *only* endorphins giving life to his eyes.

Jonathan shrugs. "It's the first landmark that came to mind. It's close, but still far enough for a good workout." He tips his head back, finishing off the water.

"Good for you. I think this new hobby is great. Exercise is good for the mind, body, and spirit." Standard Dad passes us one more time, patting Jonathan on the back again, before he addresses me. "Hey, kiddo, this is pretty early for you, isn't it?"

I nod at him. "Yeah, I have a school project."

He shouts a variety of sayings from chapter 7: "Salutations and Farewells" and is out the door. I find myself alone in the kitchen with my brother, who is sober, pleasant, and now, well hydrated.

"Jonathan?"

He sits down at the breakfast nook, a foot propped up so he can massage his calf, and stares at me, waiting. Here he is, giving me his undivided attention. But of course, I can't stay. I have to meet Henry at Ludwig's so we can get our interview over with.

"I—I'll see you this afternoon, okay?"

"Okay," he says, and I hope that's the same as him promising he's not going to hide in his room today.

CHAPTER
FIFTEEN

Henry's already at Ludwig's when I arrive.

The owner, whose name is actually Antonio—Ludwig is his wife's father, and Antonio married into the doughnut business—greets me with a robust handshake.

"Amanda, welcome! Henry tells me you don't like doughnuts."

Henry smiles at me before taking a big bite out of a croissant. Antonio hands me one and I hesitantly bite into it, afraid of encountering something like marmalade or chocolate in the center. Pleasantly I find ham, egg, and cheese.

"Let's go over here, in the booth, out of everyone's way."

Contrary to what one would suspect about the owner of a

shop selling primarily baked goods, Antonio is much taller than he is wide. We follow him through the cluster of mismatched chairs and tables to the back of the shop, proving that this store is actually bigger than the storefront indicates. Henry and I sit at a blue vinyl booth. Antonio sits across from us, resting his arm over the top of the backrest.

Antonio is obviously as bored with our questions as we are and tosses out short answers to the usual suspects, i.e., how long have you been in business? He's more interested in telling us about the product, capping off every sentence with, "If only you would try it," and then pausing to grin at us, like surely one of his descriptions is going to make us change our minds about our mutual aversion to doughnuts. Like we're this close to exclaiming, "A bacon doughnut with a maple-syrup glaze, you say? That I have to try!"

"We have a seasonal Garfield High football doughnut. The Chocolate Touchdown. We could do one for soccer." He nods at Henry, who, per usual, is sporting his Garfield High Soccer Windbreaker.

"An Out-on-Injury éclair."

I find myself hanging on every word as Henry describes the summer pickup game that messed up his knee.

"We even have a scone in honor of Grace Marlamount," Antonio says. "You both went to school with her, didn't you?"

"You do?" Henry asks. How he's found his voice after this revelation, I'm not sure.

"Yeah," Antonio says. "The Boo-Berry scone."

"The—" Henry starts, glancing at me. "What?"

Antonio laughs, but he's got this distant look in his eyes, a sad smile on his lips. "She used to come in here all the time when she was a kid. Hell, even when she was a newborn. I grew up with her mom, so I'd always throw in a free coffee. Gracie loved anything blueberry, but she couldn't say it. Boo-berry muffin. Boo-berry bagel. Boo-berry scone. Maggie and I thought it was so funny, we never corrected her."

Maggie. Margaret Marlamount. Grace's mom.

"One day they came in," he continues, "when she was around six, I think, and she started saying it the right way. Figured it out on her own. That's what happens, though; kids grow up."

It's visible on his face, the passing thought that kids grow up, but Grace will not. Not anymore.

"She didn't come in here much when she got older," Antonio says. "Occasionally, she'd stop by with a friend or two. I'd tease her about the boo-berry, and she'd tease me right back, rolling her eyes and telling me to find a new joke."

There's joy in his soft laughter, even though his eyes are welling with tears.

"Aw, hey, man, I'm sorry," Antonio says, nodding at Henry before getting up briefly to retrieve napkins from the counter.

I glance at Henry. He has his fingers pressed into his eyes. He moves them away and sniffles. Tears are streaming down his cheeks.

Antonio drops a small pile of napkins in front of Henry. "I shouldn't have—I mean, it wasn't that long ago that she . . ."

"It's okay," Henry says, wiping his cheeks, rubbing out the tears that have latched onto his eyelashes. "It's nice to hear stories about her." He pauses for a moment to grab another napkin from the stack. "She used to have sleepovers with my sister, and they would sometimes make blueberry pancakes in the morning." A smile passes over his lips but doesn't stay long. "They never turned out very well."

The image I get from this, Sutton and Grace, two girls braiding each other's hair, hiding behind their pillows watching scary movies, their pajamas getting covered in flour while they baked in the morning—is wrong, I think. It must be. Sleepovers in their case followed parties that lasted until sunrise. They were more like crash pads, somewhere to sleep it off. I forget that they were regular friends, too. Friends before the party, after the party, during the party, away from the party. Friends first, all the rest second.

"I bet she ate them anyway?" Antonio says. "Too much pride, that one—she never would have admitted they were bad."

"She picked out the blueberries," Henry says.

Antonio is still shaking his head at the loss. Still smiling at her memory. And now his cheeks are wet, too.

My throat constricts, like I might join them in crying at what's turned out to be a very depressing breakfast, but instead I manage a sympathetic smile.

"It breaks my heart," I say, being especially careful not to look at Henry.

It's not safe for me to cry here. Because what if Antonio remembers our last names, and any second now he realizes who I am? What if *Maggie* still comes in here all the time? I can't be caught crying, I have to be ready to offer condolences.

We wrap up the questions quickly after that, and Antonio sends us home with a box full of doughnuts to share with our class.

All I can get out of Henry as we leave Ludwig's are one-word answers, sometimes not even full words, just *hmm*s and *mm*s, practically grunts.

"I can drop the doughnuts off with Mr. Scott," I offer, holding out my hands, ready to take the box from him. "My first class is right by his room."

Henry sets the box on top of his car while he opens the door, ignoring me completely now.

"Fine," I say, turning away. "See you at school, then." I don't even make it a step before his voice has me spinning back around.

"That was some performance, Amanda." He's standing there, one elbow resting on his open door, squinting against the morning sun. "I know you're not that cold."

I give him a loose shrug. "Just because I didn't cry?"

He bites down on the corner of his lip and concentrates his

gaze on his forearm. "Didn't," he says, "or wouldn't?"

"Couldn't."

His eyes flash up at me. After a moment he's shaking his head, opening his mouth with a couple of false starts. He wants to speak but doesn't know what to say.

"Why won't you cry?" he finally asks.

No one ever questions why I'm not crying, and they shouldn't. I'm the comfort, I'm not the tears. Their sadness is heavier than mine, and they know it. Everyone lost someone. I'm the only person who got someone back nearly intact. And since Jonathan appears remorseless, I have to be the face that repents.

"Would it make you feel better if I cried?"

At this, his expression switches from confused to stunned. "Yes," he says. "Okay? Yes."

"And how do you think that would've made Antonio feel?"

"What are you talking about?"

"Come on, Henry," I say calmly, because getting angry over this makes me defensive, and I cannot be that either, not when it comes to Jonathan. I won't make that mistake again, like I did when he cornered me the night of homecoming. "The poor man was sitting there passing out napkins, reminiscing about Grace when she was a baby, and the sister of the guy who ended her life sits across from him *crying*—do you think he'd believe my tears were for Grace?"

"Yes."

"No," I say at the same time. "He'll think they're for my degenerate sociopath of a brother." I borrow words from articles used to describe Jonathan. *Degenerate. Sociopath.* They never used the word *brother*. "He'll think they're for the crappy way I must feel being related to someone like that. And then it's no longer about Grace, is it?"

"That's—that's preposterous."

"It isn't, though. And you proved my point when you told me to cry."

"I told you to cry because you looked like you wanted to fucking have a cry!"

I shake my head. My stiff upper lip has been perfected to appear as empathy and nothing more; I don't believe he saw through it.

"You wanted me to cry because it would make you feel better. *You.* Most people are the opposite; most people don't want to see Jonathan Tart's little sister hamming it up over the accident that he was entirely responsible for."

"You're for real, aren't you?"

I can't fathom why he's looking at me like he thinks I've lost it.

He shrugs and shakes his head, but keeps his voice calm, too. "So . . . what do you think they want, then? From you?"

"An apology."

"An apology for . . . who? For him?"

I nod, and he comes toward me, leaving his door wide open,

and not stopping this time until he's standing right in front of me. "No one has to be sorry for what Jonathan did except Jonathan."

"You're lucky," I say, staring into his eyes. "You actually believe that."

He doesn't try to stop me when I walk away.

CHAPTER
SIXTEEN

Sutton always wore a miniskirt and a pout, and people fought to make her smile, though only two were ever successful: Grace and Jonathan. Grace was the envy of everyone in the room, made worse because she didn't seem to have any idea. Jonathan was at the center of it all.

There was champagne, and whiskey—Jonathan's favorite—and an entire bathtub full of beer cans. There were games. Kings cup and flip cup and quarters and hockey and asshole and high or low. There were shots; a line to the bathroom that extended all the way into the living room; voices singing "Sweet Caroline" at the top of their lungs; couples that had formed within the hour making out in the basement. There was a pyramid of empties on the counter; someone throwing up in the bushes; solo dances on the dining room table; filthy phrases drawn with marker on those who were unfortunate enough to have been among the first to pass out.

It could have been any night.

I was pacing in the hallway at Sylvia's graduation party, waiting. He arrived quicker than I thought he would, but also not fast enough.

"What are you doing over here all alone?" he'd said. "Not in the party mood?"

I was sure he knew that if it weren't for him, I'd have left hours ago. The moment Blake put his arm around Dawn and her face lit up, full voltage, and I heard Jonathan's whiskey-soaked laugh, too smug and too clever for anyone's good, I would've gone home and put myself to bed with my laptop and a movie.

I wasn't afraid of missing anything at the party. I was afraid of missing him.

"I'm sorry," I said. "I thought alone was exactly how you wanted me."

I liked watching the shock pass over him at my flirty comment, complete with popping eyes and a jaw-dropping smile. I'd never been so brazen in my whole life.

"Touché," he said. There was nothing else for him to say.

"So, now what?" I cooed, laying it on thick now that I knew what it would do to his face.

"Oh, no—nice try. I'm not playing this game."

"What game?" This time my overstated pout and eyelash batting made him roll his eyes a little.

"The game where I offer up a suggestion and you shut it down." It was a game we played often—I had to give him that.

We could hear Jonathan in the other room, "Baby, stop . . . come here, you—" undoubtedly calling to Sutton, because they always *laid it on thick*, especially when there was an audience. She responded just as loudly, but what she was saying back to him was indecipherable except for the word *bastard*. Like all their fights, this one lasted two seconds and ended in Sutton giggling and Jonathan laughing, with Grace in the background saying something to them we couldn't quite make out, but knew from past encounters was probably either *Get a room!* or *Get a therapist.*

"I don't want us to be like them," I blurted out. I was no longer the girl who could shock him, and he was no longer the boy who made my stomach flip. We were ourselves again.

Henry joined me where I leaned against the wall, slouching down so our shoulders were pressed together. "We won't."

We won't be as bad as Jonathan and Sutton, we declared that night. *We won't call each other baby. We won't grind on each other in public. We'll trust each other. We'll have real conversations. We'll have the kind of passion that doesn't override us*—though that night, we forgot about the last one.

The first time we dared kiss we were alone in that hallway with the party, our siblings laughing and shouting on the other side of the wall, my head pressed uncomfortably against the side of a picture frame, Henry's hands tentatively on my shoulders. We got better at it.

"I want to get out of here," I said.

"For once, we agree."

We left the party, running and sliding on wet pavement, on our way to Henry's car as the rain poured on us.

It felt like we were the only two people left in the whole world once we got back to my empty house and headed upstairs to get out of our wet clothes. I made Henry turn around while I changed, and he undressed right in front of me, since being brazen was nothing new to him.

"I think I've probably wanted this for a very long time," he confessed when we were both in dry sweats and nestled in my bed, in the dark quiet, with just the sound of our voices and the rain beating against the window.

"Me too."

"Really? Since when—?"

"*Henry*. I don't know the exact moment."

"You should think about it," he said. "Then, when it comes to you, I'll tell you mine."

"You know the exact moment?" Immediately, I got combative. "No, you don't."

He found me in the darkness and pulled me closer. "I do too, and one day I'll tell you. But only when it's an even trade."

He kissed me before I could tell him that he had a deal.

We kissed the rest of the night, all night, until we fell asleep tangled together under the covers of my bed.

I woke up the next morning to hazy light, my phone vibrating against the nightstand, and Henry nowhere in sight.

Like it had all been a dream.

CHAPTER SEVENTEEN

I tell Graham I want to skip sixth period. And in true Graham fashion, he gets us out of class by telling the school administrator we're a part of the Clean Up Campus program, and we need notes to be excused to collect trash by the tennis courts. Which is exactly what we end up doing, as it's impossible for Graham to lie.

I hold the bag, Graham picks up the trash. We both wear bright-green sanitation gloves. Still, it's better than being in class with Henry after what happened at Ludwig's this morning.

"What would I do without you?" I say, watching him smile. I slowly step closer and closer to him, and his smile gets bigger; he knows what I'm doing.

"You don't have a personal space bubble at all, do you?" he says when my foot brushes against his.

"Not when it comes to you I don't." I take another step in sync with his, and since it's not possible for him to bend forward to pick up trash with me right here, he stops walking. I step in front of him and kiss him, and pull him toward me until his hands end up around my waist.

"Do you remember our first kiss?" he says, turning red as I nod. "Under the stars," he says.

It was three days after we dropped Jonathan off at prison, and I was a mess of snot and tears, and wearing my ugly winter fleece pajamas, but Graham remembers the stars. I would spend this entire hour kissing him just for that, but we said we would pick up trash, so that's what we continue doing.

Two gusts of wind later, he asks, "So how are things at home?"

It feels a bit like he's following a protocol for how to deal with your girlfriend when her brother returns from prison and she hasn't wanted to talk about it with you, but is more than happy to fight about it with Henry Crane. Step One: relax girlfriend by returning her kisses; Step Two: bring up a happy memory; Step Three: broach the subject again carefully with a broad statement.

"You mean, how are things with Jonathan?" I call him out.

He nods, looking at the grape soda he's dumping out instead of at me. When he finally does look at me, his stare is so caring and sincere, I feel bad that I haven't brought it up with him sooner.

"Do you remember what he was like before . . . everything?"

Graham shakes his head. "I didn't really know him. I mean, he was older. . . ."

And the only underclassman Jonathan hung out with was Grace. Graham doesn't say it, but I know he's thinking it.

"But you knew what he was like." Everyone did.

"Yeah, I guess. He was supposed to be fun, sort of crazy . . . wild."

"That's not what I mean."

"Well, what do you mean?"

"He was . . ." *Thoughtful*, I think. So thoughtful that when he told you a joke it was as though it'd been tailored just for you. And genuine—he said something to you, he meant it, he was good for it, he'd fight for it and for you, too. And warm. He was inviting in a way that no one in my family is, including me.

Sociopath is the word the article in *Time* used to describe him.

I want Graham to see more than that, more than someone who was able to manipulate his way into everyone's heart. I want to explain to Graham that "things at home," the way Jonathan is now, are bleak, and growing worse every day because he doesn't act like his old self—except for the times when he shouldn't.

"Hey." Graham peels off his gloves so he can tuck his hand under my chin and force me to look at him when he tells me, "It's not your fault," for the billionth time.

This time I say, "But I was there."

"Jonathan was going to do whatever he wanted. His decisions are his own." He goes on. It's the same spiel he's given me many times before, one he knows so well he could even slur it at me when he was wasted at the homecoming after-party.

It piggybacks off Dawn's reasoning: *I was with Blake and you were with Henry, and how could we have known?* And thinking about all of it together, and my fight with Henry, presents me with the haunting thought that this front I put up, it might be for me more than it is for other people.

CHAPTER
EIGHTEEN

"**T**oday was an absolutely terrible, no good, very bad day."
This is how Dawn answers the phone when I call her
in the bathroom during lunch on Thursday. She rattles on about
her probably-definitely failed bio quiz, and how she's sure the
chicken she just ate was undercooked. And I find myself laughing, but mostly wishing I was there laughing with her, in person.

"I told Becky I was going to get salmonella, and she was like,
'Can't you only get that from salmon?'" Dawn says.

We share another laugh, and I realize that it's not just the
two of us laughing. There is a third person there laughing just as
hard as we are. *Becky.*

Becky is Dawn's replacement roommate after her first

roommate was too homesick to stay in Santa Barbara and went back to Iowa after just two weeks. First Roommate was very quiet, and the unofficial president of the Elvis Fan Club, and she covered her entire side of the dorm room with posters and kept a cardboard cutout of Gold Lamé Elvis stashed in the closet. Replacement Roommate Becky, Dawn and I suspected, would be just as weird in her own way. And she was—dyeing her hair what she called Beach Bottle Blond because she wanted to "embrace beach culture," always complaining about how Santa Barbara is colder and wetter than the Phoenix climate she'd been used to all her life, and constantly consuming pickles because she read somewhere that they would shrink her stomach. But more and more I've noticed her there, laughing with Dawn on the other end of the line.

"How are you?" Dawn asks. "Are you still avoiding Henry, or are you actually going to class today?" Dawn sees my point and agrees with me about not crying in front of certain people, and especially not in front of my fellow Garfield High students or anyone who had known Grace since she was a newborn. It's always nice to have to her support, and I guess Becky's too—I can hear her saying something in the background. She's definitely putting on a British accent.

"So what happened with your test? I thought you liked bio," I say, to change the subject.

"The problem isn't bio, the problem is Becky and I went to a frat party last night and had too many Jell-O shots."

There are so many clichés in this sentence, I can't even

believe it's Dawn delivering the lines.

I listen to them laugh, listen to all the "guess you had to be there" jokes, and pretend that soon this will all be mine. I never thought I wanted frat parties and Jell-O shots, but they have got to be better than what I have now.

CHAPTER
NINETEEN

"*N*ice of you to join us today," Henry greets me when I walk into sixth period after hanging up with Dawn . . . and Becky. He's strangely upbeat given that yesterday I stormed off in another one of my "huffs."

"I was picking up trash."

"Is that what the kids are calling it these days?" he jokes, light as ever—practically sucking up, like he feels bad about yesterday morning. I was too honest with him again; I should not have told him that I'm careful about crying; shouldn't have explained it to him; shouldn't have been foolish enough to believe that he'd understand; and definitely shouldn't have been so damn adamant about proving him wrong when he didn't.

"I finished the project," he says. "You're welcome to check it over, but it's mostly quoting Antonio."

He tosses me the printed and stapled assignment, complete with the interview and an analysis of it.

"Thank you," I say, because it really is done well. And it's not even due until tomorrow.

He shrugs off my gratitude, repositioning himself so he's facing me. "I've been thinking."

"Alert the press."

"About what you were saying, outside Ludwig's."

There are so many places he could go with this. My heart ramps up to some ungodly number of beats per minute as I wait for him to continue.

"What you said, about being sorry . . ."

Now I'm certain I've said too much. I turn away from him, staring at the window, where a tree is being pushed up against the glass by the wind, wishing I were outside this room. Henry puts a hand on my wrist, bringing me back.

"I don't think you should feel responsible at all. Not for Jonathan, and especially not for how people feel about him."

Since I feel responsible, Henry must think I believe he should feel responsible, too. Even though Sutton wasn't the one behind the wheel. I try to see through him the way he seems to so effortlessly see through me. I try to interpret how much of this conversation is hiding his own guilt. But I can't read him.

"Responsibility is a tricky thing, Henry."

He does nothing to show me he agrees, but doesn't protest either.

I try to explain it so he'll understand. "Have you ever heard of 'diffusion of responsibility'?"

Henry shakes his head.

"The diffusion of responsibility states that people feel less inclined to take responsibility for something if others are present. I learned about it in gym, when they were teaching us about self-defense," I tell him. "If we're ever attacked in public, we're supposed to single someone out to help us. Like screaming, 'Man in blue shirt, help me up,' or 'Woman with eye patch, come to my rescue.' Otherwise, no one might help us."

"That's messed up." He eyes me warily, but I keep going. Right now it really does seem like if I can explain it correctly, he'll understand where I'm coming from. And I realize what's really making me more talkative than I've been in months with anyone besides Dawn is that I'm hoping—I'm desperate—for him to tell me why all my reasoning, all the ways I've come up with to explain why I'm guilty, are wrong. He'll punch holes in my argument like he's done so many times before, and this time I'm craving that.

"I think that because there were so many of us at Sylvia's," I continue, "and there's so much blame to go around, that everyone gets only a small piece. It's so light, it feels like nothing."

He picks up before I can keep going. "If we're supposed to be responsible for everyone around us, all the time, then why are we sitting here talking? Why aren't we checking in on patrons at a bar, taking their keys? Or stopping the homeless person on the corner from shooting up?"

"Not *everyone* around us."

It passes over his face in a wave of dread, the realization that no one should have had to tell us to watch out for them; not that night or any other. Jonathan and Sutton were ours—Henry's and mine. Our family. It's a torturous thought, but there it is. I finally allow myself to have it properly, while he's having it too; it doesn't seem so excruciating now that we're sharing it. If anyone was supposed to be looking out for them, it was us.

Henry touches my wrist again. This time, he's slower to remove it. I allow myself only a second to think about what it'd be like to reach out and grab his hand, but his hand is gone in a flash, folded in front of him on his desk. "Maybe we were being selfish," he says. "But we were also entirely clueless. We're just not as ignorant anymore."

It wasn't the rebuttal I was hoping for, because there is no other way to see it. Selfish—yes. Clueless—entirely. Ignorance was bliss, it really was.

"Maybe no one is," he continues. "Even if now they have to be sad."

There's a hitch in his voice, and he looks down at the desk.

Mr. Scott stands in front of the class and asks for our attention so he can go over review items for our quiz next week. Perfect timing, for once.

Texting with Dawn, Thursday, 6:34 p.m.

Standard Dad is at a loss over dinner.

Isn't he always?

He wants Jonathan to get a job and go back to school. Not necessarily in that order.

Mumsy thinks it's all happening too fast.

"Stop pressuring him!"—Mumsy. Because the only kind of pressure Mumsy approves of is the kind that happens when her Pilates class breaks out the resistance tubes.

Your parents crack me up.

It's all very tense, actually. Jonathan just described his parole officer as "trite and unfitting."

Ah, so he's got his grown-up voice on. Such a manipulator. ☺ Is it working? Wait—are you texting at the table?

Haha, it's working. It always does. But Mumsy is still glaring at Standard Dad. It's fine, no one notices what I do, remember? ☺

Then you should take off and come visit me for a week.

I'll get right on that.

CHAPTER
TWENTY

After dinner, Jonathan, my father, and I clean up and load the dishwasher while Mumsy goes upstairs to lie down.

"I'm going for a jog," Jonathan announces when we're done.

"At this hour?" Standard Dad glances at his watch.

It's barely eight o'clock, though it's been dark for hours.

"Or I could just drive you to Starbucks," I say, eyeing Jonathan so he'll know I'm onto him.

"Coffee, *at this hour?*" My dad shakes his head. *How crazy are my kids?*

"If you don't mind," Jonathan says to me. He's already reached the front door.

I do mind. I have a calculus quiz to study for, but I'm curious about why Jonathan wants to see this Wren girl again and what they could possibly have to say to each other.

"So you know Wren's schedule now, huh?" I ask the second we're in the car.

"It's been over twelve hours without someone complimenting me on my eyes. I have to get my fix."

"Your eyes are breathtaking."

He doesn't really smile at my joke, and neither do I.

"Do you like her or something?"

He leans forward, so I can't see his face.

I try to picture if Wren is someone Jonathan would have been interested in before the accident. The answer is yes. And since he's not with Sutton, why not?

Still, I ask, "Have you talked to Sutton?"

"My phone is out of commission, remember? Mumsy is taking me to get a new one tomorrow, with a new number. But no, I will not be getting in touch with her."

"Why not?"

He's quiet until the next stop sign. "Sutton doesn't want to talk to me. Even if she thinks she does."

"What if she needs closure?"

"It won't bring her closure. Nothing will."

I don't know what to say to this, so I let the silence fill up the car until we arrive at Starbucks.

Sitting here with Jonathan and Wren is undeniably

uncomfortable. We're in the mock living room part of Starbucks. Jonathan and Wren are across from each other in plush green chairs; I'm tacked on to their little scene, perched on a stool.

"Nice to see you not dripping in sweat," Wren says.

I picture the old Jonathan smirking, brooding at her, covering my eyes to shield me from anything that would make me say "Ew."

Wren stares expectantly, like that's what she's picturing, too. But now that we're here, Jonathan barely seems happy to see her.

"How's your tea?" she asks, stripping off her apron and the black long-sleeved T-shirt she'd been wearing to reveal a black low-cut tank top and arms colored with tattoos. It's a useless question, since our tea is still too hot to drink and is sitting in front of us, untouched.

After a few seconds, Jonathan mumbles, "Not strong enough."

Wren stands up, then disappears behind the counter.

Jonathan tries to take a sip of his tea. The way his face puckers tells me it's still too hot to be drinking.

Wren comes back holding a beat-up black purse. She reaches inside and tosses Jonathan something shiny. A flask. "Jack Daniel's. Your favorite."

He shrugs. "What the hell," he says, unscrewing the top.

"Jonathan . . ." I try not to sound like a nagging mother. I fail. I want to scold them both, since this seems to be an obvious exchange: my brother's attention for alcohol. But it occurs to me that anyone could know his favorite alcohol type if they search his name. Articles like to point out that Jonathan, at just eighteen, already had a preference in alcohol type. However she's learned it, it does not sit well with me.

He pours the whiskey until his cup is so full he's going to have to slurp his first few sips without moving the cup.

"It's fine," he says to me. "I've already turned in my urine this week." His visits will be weekly for the first month or so. This still seems really risky to me.

"My cousin hates his probation officer," Wren says. "He's so demanding." She gets an almost smile out of Jonathan. "What does yours want you to do?" she asks.

Jonathan tries for another sip of his tea and is more successful this time. "For me to be a model citizen. Develop a routine. Get a job. Go to AA meetings."

I wait for signs that red flags are popping up in Wren's head. But her smile is as big as ever now.

"AA?" She shakes her head. "Well, if you're an alcoholic, you're definitely a *functioning* one."

The way she says the word *functioning* makes me look away.

When I imagine an alcoholic, my brother—now or before—is not what I see. An alcoholic is someone who has beer with breakfast and is drunk by dinner. My brother drank in excess because his life was a party. And now? What's a little Jack Daniel's while complaining about your probation officer? Or a few sips of whiskey to take the edge off when you're alone in your room with enough grief and guilt to sustain a lifetime of misery?

"Don't forget he wants you to speak to the community," I

chime in—anything to break up their game of eye lust.

"You should definitely get on board with that," Wren says.

"Why?" I say, surprised she agrees, since she was so opposed to everything else.

At the same time, Jonathan says, "Oh, I don't know."

"For the haters," she says.

The who?

"To show them how great you're doing and stuff. You're the only person who's honest about all this shit. Maybe you could get bigger gigs—gigs that would actually pay you."

"Who says I'm doing great?" Jonathan says. He quickly follows it up with, "It'd certainly be an improvement to have a payday."

"Gary wants you to have a payday, too. From a real job," I say. There's annoyance in my voice. This is the kind of payday Wren should be encouraging. Right? If you're interested in someone, as Wren is so clearly interested in my brother, you don't want him going back to jail. You don't bring him alcohol that's in direct violation of his probation. You don't encourage him to turn his community service into a paid gig.

"You're doing fucking amazing," Wren says, talking over me and leaning out of her chair to be closer to Jonathan. "You did your time. No one can touch you."

Jonathan nods along, letting out, "You're right, you're right."

Not right. But I don't say anything this time. It could be that Jonathan's placating her. We'll laugh about this later—*what was she saying about haters?* I wonder if he's amusing himself. Or if he's desperate for the company. Maybe he needs someone new and different, who didn't know Grace or what she was to him, and can't see that far down into his sadness. Maybe it doesn't matter that Wren's fascinated with his tumultuous past and helps him violate his probation, because talking to Wren is a hundred times better than a circle of recovering addicts at AA or a probation officer with a clipboard and one-size-fits-all instructions.

Maybe this is exactly what he's missing.

"Nice ink," he says, letting his eyes trail down her arms.

"Yeah, you like it?"

"It's interesting."

Her smile could eat his, but at least he's smiling.

"Do you have any?" she asks, tracing a bird outline on her forearm.

"Just one."

"You got a tattoo in prison?" The words rush out of me. The two of them seem to find my reaction amusing.

"No." Jonathan laughs. "Before."

"Let's see it," Wren says.

My eyes pore over him, searching for a hint of ink peeking out of his collar or his sleeve.

Jonathan shakes his head. "I don't think so."

"Where is it?" Wren says, her eyes poring over him, too.

He turns to me. "You really thought I'd get a tattoo in prison?" He laughs again.

"My cousin got a tattoo in prison," Wren says. She lets her hair out of its bun and shakes out the mess of kinky curls. Jonathan doesn't hide that he's watching her. "The outline of a car. It looks like shit."

"What kind of car?" Jonathan asks.

"I think it's supposed to be a Chevelle. But it looks more like a limousine to me."

The mental image of this is pretty funny. Jonathan laughs, and so do I.

"It's ironic, too," she continues. "His charge was grand theft auto."

"Don't tell me he stole a Chevelle?" Jonathan says.

Wren nods, rolls her eyes, laughs.

"Good taste, at least," Jonathan says. I've never known him to be into cars.

"It was red with white racing stripes and everything."

"Classic."

"Yeah, but you know the thing about those cars?"

Jonathan watches as she redoes her bun.

I know the answer to this, so I say, "They're really loud."

"Exactly," Wren says. "And that's how he got caught. One of the guys he stole it from heard him driving it and was like, 'Hey, that's not your car.'"

"No," I say.

At the same Jonathan says, "You're kidding."

"No, that's really what happened." She covers her mouth as a loud cackle rolls out. "I mean, what kind of a genius takes the lifted car back for a joyride around the neighborhood he stole it from?"

The three of us are doubled over at this point. Laughter like this, relieved and free-flowing, seems unnatural on Wren, breaking up her usual batting eyes and twisted grins and bringing color to her cheeks. It reminds me of the way Sutton's face used to open up when she was laughing with my brother or Grace. It was the only time she really looked approachable. The story goes that on the first day of Grace's freshman year, Sutton and she were both waiting in the counselor's office to have their schedules changed, when Grace said something that made Sutton crack up so hard Diet Coke came out of her nose, and they were inseparable ever since.

"Everyone I know who's gone to jail, it's always been for something stupid," Wren tells us when the laughter has died down.

Jonathan averts his stare, tracing his finger along the top of his cup. He's no longer leaning in her direction. I hope Wren feels like crawling under a rock. *"Everyone."* All these ex-cons she knows who didn't have to commit vehicular manslaughter to earn their bad-boy stripes.

"Lighten up," she says. She reaches out her foot and pokes him in the shin until he looks at her.

"This is as light as it gets," he tells her.

This is the saddest thing I've heard him say out loud in a long time. I think Wren will melt with sympathy. But there's a fierce look in her eyes, a smirk playing on her lips. *Challenge accepted.*

When we leave a little while later, Jonathan's the one to tell her, "I'll see you tomorrow."

He looks like he could smile once we're in the car. He doesn't, but he seems peaceful instead of exhausted. I'd blame it on the Jack Daniel's if I hadn't already seen him like this the other morning after his run.

This—*she*—is what's gotten into him.

CHAPTER
TWENTY-ONE

I barrel down the stairs on Friday night when the doorbell rings. Not fast enough, though. Standard Dad answers the door first and spouts some typical lines from the manual to Graham. Chapter 10: "What to Say to That Dude Dating Your Daughter." This entails him clearing this throat a million times, as if everything he says has another connotation.

"Great costume. But what are you supposed to be?" Standard Dad says curiously when he sees what I'm wearing. It's just a black dress. It's still surprising to see me dressed up for a non-homecoming event, I know—of course he assumes it's a costume.

"It's a black-and-white party," I explain. Halloween or not, this party is a tradition that the soccer team will not let go.

"You look great," he says. He nods again, noticing that Graham's wearing slacks.

"Good," I say, wiping at my forehead like I was worried. It makes both him and Graham laugh. I think it's a nice dress, and Dawn said she liked it when I modeled it for her via video chat. Becky liked it, too.

"Why a black-and-white party?" my dad asks. He even scratches his head.

I roll my eyes. "It's the soccer team's party. Black and white, like a soccer ball."

"Very clever." But Standard Dad doesn't sound too enthused, since That Dude Dating His Daughter is still standing right there.

There's a gap in the conversation where I think Graham wants to say, "I'll have her home by midnight" but sticks with, "Good night" instead. He blushes. If he does have me home by midnight, it's because that's when his parents want *him* home.

"Are you coming home tonight?" A Standard Dad line he never uses.

"I—I think so," I say.

Graham nods, licking his lips and popping his knuckles with his thumb.

"I'll have her home by two," he says.

I take his sweaty hand and lead him outside.

I'm surprised to see it's not Graham's car out front; the two of us climb in the backseat of the blue sedan.

That's how it works at this particular party. I forgot until now. It's an initiation of sorts. The seniors are allowed to go crazy—this gathering is for them, a last hurrah—and the other teammates live to serve them, forced to act as their personal waiters and chauffeurs. Per tradition, the underclassmen are required to dress in Hawaiian shirts, complete with leis and sunscreen smeared white across their noses.

The house hosting the party is decorated with black-and-white streamers, with a few of those blow-up palm trees placed randomly throughout the house. Halloween shows itself in the form of carved pumpkins and cobwebs. Graham and I are by far the most boring, just dressed as fancy versions of ourselves. A lot of the other senior soccer players and their dates have combined the black-and-white theme with Halloween and are dressed in skeleton suits or as referees or convicts in black-and-white stripes. The girls are donning French maid costumes or black cat ears with whiskers painted on their cheeks. Even some of the underclassmen soccer players have fake blood splattered across their Hawaiian shirts and are claiming to be Scarface.

I'm sort of at a frat party, I text Dawn.

You haven't been to a frat party until you've been to a frat party, she texts back.

So, fine. I'll never know about the fun she's having until I'm having it, too.

The thing this party and frat parties—I presume—have in common is that the second I arrive, I wish I were anywhere else.

The seniors are being sucked up to, waited on, and cheered at, like everyone here is the former Jonathan Tart. You can see the entitlement in their eyes. It looks so strange on Graham, I try to forgive it. He's only doing what's expected of him.

We stand in a circle, chatting and sipping on the vodka-crans the sophomore teammates were handing out. I huddle next to Graham, trying to be as friendly and fun as everyone else.

"Stacey, where are you applying to college?" I ask.

And: "How do you think you did on that chem test, Aran?"

And: "What did you think of the game last week?"

I sound like I'm interviewing them, or worse. I am Standard Girlfriend. Except I never got a manual. Just a *How to Stand There Quietly So You Won't Be Too Awkward* pamphlet.

I try for a joke about wearing white after Labor Day, since 80 percent of the party is dressed in black. It falls flat except for a delayed courtesy laugh from Stacey.

I hear someone say, "Crane said he was coming, man. I don't know, he'll probably be here soon," and feel a relief that is completely unwarranted.

When Henry finally appears, the balloon that was my heart deflates. As much as I don't want to look at him with Imogen—one hand slung casually around her shoulders like it's actually more comfortable for him to stand with her tucked under his arm like that—I can't stop myself from stealing glances every few seconds. They're also dressed only as fancy versions of themselves.

Sometimes I get the impression that he keeps looking at me, too. It's this first drink playing tricks on me, though, I'm pretty sure of it.

Higgins, one of the poor juniors who's had to put up with this party for three years since he made the team as a freshman, comes over to give Graham and me more drinks.

Any chance to be responsibly drunk and Graham will take advantage of it. It's like homecoming all over again—and that was barely a week ago.

Graham trades his empty cup for a fresh glass of whatever Higgins gives him. I hold up my half-full drink, to indicate I don't need another.

"Are you still on your first?" Higgins asks.

Higgins and Graham are both highly confused that I've been here for nearly two hours and have yet to finish a drink.

"Get her something she likes," Graham says.

They both look at me again, eyebrows up, waiting.

"What do you like?" Higgins says.

More stares. My mind is actually blank. The desire to laugh tickles my throat.

"Whatever you want." Graham nudges me. "They've got everything."

I try to give the kind of smile that makes me seem pleased and excited about so many possibilities.

"Come on," Graham says. He takes my watery drink and hands it to Higgins. "What'll it be?"

"I'm fine with this," I say, taking it back, sipping a little, hoping my expression doesn't reveal the truth.

"You're clearly not," Graham says. He leans in close but makes no attempt to lower his voice. "You've got a ride home, so you don't have to worry about the thing I know you worry about." He slouches so we're at eye level. He looks tired, and his breath smells like a bowl of fruit that's been left out in the sun. "I know you're not huge into this kind of stuff, but I think you should . . . join in. Have fun, Amanda. You'll be surprised how much *fun* it is."

It sounds like something Jonathan would say.

He smiles, so I smile back, nodding, too, like I can't believe how right he is. His gaze drifts to the surrounding party, and mine follows. Everyone is clutching their drinks in front of them, their faces red and pinched but undeniably happy. Carefree. I wonder if it's obvious that I'm not.

I think about Grace as I look around at where people are gathered; places she should be standing, but isn't because she left the safe confines of a party just like this one and carefree slipped ominously into reckless.

"So what'll it be?" Graham says. "Well?" His smile has turned pleading. I think of his words. *Join in. You don't have to worry about the thing I know you worry about.*

Do you ever worry about it? I think. But I know the answer; of course he does. It's exactly like Jonathan said. *The party's not the problem.* And: *Only you can prevent forest fires.* And here we are with all these designated drivers. Nothing to worry about. It's that simple.

"I'll have a gin rickey," I tell him. The only drink that comes to mind.

Graham hesitates, but instead of asking me what I presume he must be thinking—*what the hell is a gin rickey?*—he says, "Okay." He turns to Higgins. "Got that?" His voice is demanding.

Higgins has one eyebrow up and a slight grimace. But he gets out his phone, flashing it for Graham. He will research this gin rickey and report back. I feel terrible for making him go the extra mile.

"Is that even a real thing?" Graham asks after he's gone.

"Oh, yes," I say. "It was F. Scott Fitzgerald's favorite drink." Which is the truth.

Graham squints at me. "How do you even know—you know what? Never mind." He tips his drink back so far as he gulps it down that the umbrella falls out.

"It's all I could think of. . . ." But Graham's head is already turned; he's waving someone over. We're surrounded by others in seconds, but I feel more alone than ever, like I'm the only student at Garfield High who is completely lost and not having a good time.

My eyes fall on Henry across the room, and he's looking back at me.

What Higgins brings me is gin and Sprite with two lime wedges floating in it, which he claims is technically the same as a gin rickey. Honestly I wouldn't know the difference. I take a large swig and try to smile appreciatively, even though I've instantly concluded that gin rickey is entirely the wrong name for this drink. Sparkling Pine-Sol would be a more accurate fit. I mean, it's really terrible. With every sip I think: this, *this*, must've been what Sutton was drinking that night she threw up in our driveway; what my brother was drinking on his eighteenth birthday when I found him on the bathroom floor with his hand in the toilet.

I sip slowly. Graham drinks like he's trying to win a contest. But the more he drinks, the more he forgets that I'm depressing and starts thinking that I'm the "most fun, most prettiest girl in the room." And then, after a while, he's having so much fun he forgets I exist at all, and I can walk away.

I go outside to the far side of the house, by a woodpile and a wheelbarrow full of succulents. Light from the driveway makes it brighter back here than I'd like, but for the purpose of dumping out the large remainder of my imitation gin rickey, I think it will do the trick. When Henry comes around the corner, right behind me, I'm not surprised. He's all in black too—black slacks, black dress shoes, black soccer Windbreaker.

Maybe it was those five sips of faux gin rickey, but I really believe that Henry was waiting to catch me alone.

I accidentally smile when I see him. He does the same thing, turning his head as if that will hide it from me.

"I can take you home, if you want," he says.

"Uh-oh, another failed attempt at hiding what a depressive mess I am."

"It's not that. You just seem like you're ready to go." He looks away when he tells me, "I've only had one bottle of this

vitamin-infused water—which is awful, in case you were wondering."

"Are you sidelined from partying with the soccer team, too?"
A lame joke, but he still rewards me with a laugh.

"Imogen has decided to drink enough for the both of us,"
he says.

My insides shudder at the way her name sounds coming out
of his mouth, with that accent.

"And Graham is drinking the rest," he says, peeking at me
with a smirk.

I allow myself a real smile. Henry won't care if it still seems
sad.

We're quiet for a while. "Higgins is going to give me a ride,"
I say.

"All right," he says. The conversation feels over, but neither
of us goes anywhere.

Time passes, and we stand there, not quite looking at each
other, but my entire body is aware of his presence. I don't know
how long we remain like this, and I don't care.

"Can I confess that sometimes all I can think is: why?"
Henry blurts out. "Why did it have to happen, and why that
night . . . ?"

"We should have kept fighting with each other," I con-
clude.

"And then what?" he says. Mocking laughter swells out of
him. I wonder if he's had this conversation with himself many
times before. "We'd have saved them all?"

I shake my head and shrug, and he does the same. The thing is, we don't really know.

We leave behind a millions selves, a herd of them who have moved on without us, making different decisions. There's a version of me who said, "No, I don't want to," when Dawn was just the new girl across the street who showed up at my front door with her mother, toting a Barbie, asking if I wanted to play; a version who said screw it to stage fright and tried out for *Annie*; a version who kept my growing feelings for Henry Crane buried; a version who didn't answer any of Graham's phone calls those days after Jonathan's incarceration, when he would call to check up on me; there's a version of me who never kissed him. The worse things get, the more I think about those selves and wonder if their lives are turning out better than mine.

"We could really punish ourselves with that one," Henry says, kicking at the ground.

"Aren't we already, though?" I glance around us, at the seclusion we've chosen.

"I guess," he says. "You're with Graham."

I stare at him. Baiting me, tricking me, trying to get a rise out of me—whatever he's doing, it's working. But I can shoot back. "You're with Imogen."

"*Okay.*" He smiles. "That's not the same."

"Why not?"

He puffs out his cheeks and lets his breath out slowly. "Graham is—how do they put it—a 'sucker for a fixer-upper.'"

"What the hell does that mean?"

"He likes that you're kind of a depressive mess, even if he complains about it."

"That makes total sense, Henry. *Wow*."

"I meant nothing bad by it, and I'm sure you'll scamper off to Santa Barbara and that will be that with him. No harm done. But that's why you're sticking it out. He's invested in you, so you try to invest back."

"You're infuriating. This is so typical of you, thinking you know what's going on with things that have absolutely nothing to do with you. You're not as smart as you think you are." I'm thirteen again, telling Henry to shut up and mind his own business after he asked why my brother came to see me at the science fair instead of my parents. I'm back at the homecoming after-party. And outside Ludwig's. Henry forces me to defend the parts of my life I have no defense for.

"And Imogen is the most obvious person you could have chosen," I add. "Talk about willing and able."

"Okay, okay. Leave her out of this, please."

The way he sticks up for her makes my bones ache, like they've shattered into a million pieces and I'm going to whoosh into the ground any second.

"How is that fair?" I say.

"Because what I said wasn't insulting to Graham, and it was the truth. You're just reaching for anything to bash Imogen with."

I don't need this. I turn to go.

"She's not you, is really what you want to say," he calls to me, and I have no choice but to pivot back around. His face has opened up; it's radiating hope. He holds out his arms, his hands in the air, mad at the world or surrendering to it, it's hard to tell. He focuses on me and gives one more shrug. "I'm sorry about that, too, all right?"

There's nowhere to keep his admission, nothing to do but let it float away. I'm leaving behind another self, the one who kisses him angrily, passionately—there's a fine line between them— and says, *Then let's* not *just forget it*.

Instead, I'm the version of myself who says, "Not all right."

My voice is so quiet I don't think he's heard, but he rubs his forehead, then tugs on the left side of his hair the way he some- times does when he's waiting for the teacher to pass out a test, or those moments when he takes his place on the soccer field before the start of a match.

"Amanda," he finally says, more to the sky than to me. Henry chooses the self who walks toward me. I listen to the twigs crack under his shoes, until he's right in front of me.

"It's useless," he says. I want to ask what he means—useless to deny what we want, or useless to give in to it—but I'm entirely too distracted by his closeness. His hands trail up past my shoul- ders, my neck. He holds my face and kisses me until I'm kissing him back, stumbling against the woodpile, and then, pressed up against the side of the house. It's almost too much. I think I might be gripping him really hard, but I don't care. It wasn't like this the last time we kissed, when I'd thought I'd get to do it a hundred more times.

I don't think about anything else outside of how much I want this, how good it feels. I don't think of Graham or Imogen. I don't think about the rest of the party. I don't think about Jonathan or Sutton or Grace.

CHAPTER
TWENTY-TWO

G raham is drunk and ready to leave by the time I make it back to the party. Even if I do look as guilty as I feel, he's not going to pick up on it.

"You're okay to drive us?" I ask Higgins as we follow him out to his car.

"He's fine," Graham boasts, slapping Higgins on the back so hard Higgins drops the keys. "He knows what happens to the guys who break the rules of the black-and-white party."

I almost ask, *What happens?* But I probably don't want to know anyway.

Higgins turns to me and says, "I promise, I'm okay to drive."

Graham is sloppy, and he doesn't wear inebriation well. One eye is almost closed, one side of his mouth reels back whenever he speaks. The halves of his face look like they don't belong to the same person. Jonathan never looked like that when he was at a party. When his eyes got heavy, they smoldered. I imagine if he ever started to look as drunk as he was, he wasn't in any condition to leave the bathroom anyway.

When Graham presses himself against me and kisses me, I taste mint. So at least he's a courteous drunk. I play like I'm bashful about kissing in front of Higgins—which I am—but Graham isn't picking up social cues. I sit back in my seat; Graham leans over me in a lazy hug, his lips plastered to my neck.

I open my eyes so I can see the road, even though I have to peer over Graham's shoulder and his mouth is cold and wet against my neck and his hands are tangled in my hair. Is Higgins really okay to drive? I thought that maybe some of the sunscreened and lei-wearing guys looked *too* happy at the party, like they were having just as good a time as the seniors. How serious is soccer team hierarchy anyway, really? I imagine what I'll do if Higgins starts to veer off to the side of the road, the way Jonathan did that night. Maybe I could break away from Graham and lunge forward and grab the wheel. Or maybe a simple, "Hey, Higgins, stay in the lines," would suffice. It hits me that Graham and I are in the backseat—me in the exact seat that Grace was in when she died.

It's weird to think about dying—it's creepy and sad. The last thing people saw of me: a girl holding a cup wet with condensation, never leaving her boyfriend's side, except for those ten minutes when she was unaccounted for.

The last time I saw Grace, she was laughing. Her hair was damp and curly, frizzy in front from the rain. She was saying something to my brother with her hands on her hips. Tugging on Sutton's strapless dress to keep it from twisting wrong and dropping too low, promising her it still looked amazing. Sipping from a plastic champagne flute with her pinkie up, cracking up over it, and covering her mouth until she swallowed.

It's too late for us if Higgins is drunk, I decide.

And it's probably all in my head, anyway—too much *awareness*.

We pull up to my house, and Higgins drums his fingers on the steering wheel, respectfully keeping his eyes averted as Graham attempts to give me a passionate kiss good-bye.

"Thank you," I call to Higgins as I climb out of the car.

He waves, at the same time Graham leans over and slurs, "I told you tonight would be epic."

Graham never lies.

CHAPTER
TWENTY-THREE

One, two, three rings; four, five, six—and Dawn's voicemail greeting is crisp in my ear. "Hi, it's Dawn"—I can hear the sound of the ocean in the background, the crashing of waves, seagulls cawing, static caused by the wind. "I'm studying hard, of course, or getting a tan at the beach!" I imagine myself there, standing in the sand in bare feet while the waves roll in, tickling my toes when they reach me. Dawn laughs at the end of her message, and I laugh with her. I don't care that I'm alone in my room, laughing to a recording like a crazy person. Sometimes you just need to laugh with your best friend. I call her back, just to listen to the message again.

She's in Los Angeles with Becky this weekend, so I don't expect her to be available.

Undeniably, part of me is relieved. Could I manage to say the words, even to her? *Henry and me*—no. It's been less than twelve hours since the party, and I can barely think them. The memory of it makes me adrenaline-awake and fidgety. And also, sorry. More than anything else, just so damn sorry.

Everything I do the rest of the day serves the very important purpose of distracting me from wondering why Henry has yet to contact me. I do more laundry than I've ever done on a weekend. I wrap up an application to the University of Michigan. I finish homework that's not due until Thursday.

I've convinced myself it was a mistake. It's over now anyway. Forgotten. A fluke in the span of our lives. A moment of weakness that can be attributed to being some of the only sober people at that party. All I should be feeling is profound relief— abundant gratitude that it hasn't carried on any further. We were releasing secrets, and that one—our unfinished feelings for each other—came spilling out, too. Then at seven thirty he sends a text.

I'm around. You should be around too.

I stand there in the middle of my room, a statue with my thumbs ready to type. *Okay* seems both too eager and too casual. *Around where?* also teeters on eager.

I type, *When?* I press send.

Now is preferable. Come over. Parents and Sutton out for the rest of the weekend.

If it were possible, my entire body would be blushing right now.

I'll be there. I sort of regret sending this, of course. But it's done. So I get in my car and drive away.

CHAPTER
TWENTY-FOUR

The first thing Henry Crane ever said to me was, "Cheerio, I'm Henry, from the UK." Seriously. Right away I thought, this is someone who's trying too hard. I could spot this kind of thing easily, even in the seventh grade, since Jonathan was the epitome of "effortless."

I'd replied with: "And when that gets old, you'll be Javier from Spain?" I'd been positive that everything about him was fake. I might've apologized once I realized he really was telling the truth. But everywhere I turned it seemed Henry was there, introducing himself with "Cheerio" and making sure to add his country of origin, as if that was the normal way to introduce yourself to people. And everyone else seemed to reward him for this. "Really? Your accent is awesome."

We disagreed about things I didn't think were even up for debate. The pronunciation of the word *often*. Whether or not the tomato is considered a vegetable. The name of the person Penny Lane was based on in the movie *Almost Famous*.

Sometimes we did find the answers; a quick internet search did the trick. But we argued about who was right the majority of the time. The score I'd tallied in my head was 18–11, me. Henry insisted it was 23–17, him.

We played pranks on each other. Freshman year, Henry took the embarrassing poster of me on display at the public library for winning an essay contest and hung it on the bulletin board in the school's main entrance.

We had ceramics class together first semester sophomore year. Henry cornered me in the art supply room the first day of school. I thought he was going to comment on my ugly vase. Instead he said, "It's getting bad, between Jonathan and Sutton."

By *bad*, he of course meant *gross*. I couldn't agree more.

"I liked it better when my sister didn't have a pet name."

"I liked it better when my brother wasn't handing out pet names to people he wasn't related to."

"You'd think he'd be more creative. Not all pet names have to have the word *baby* in them," Henry said.

A few weeks later, we walked into ceramics to find Sutton and Jonathan in the back, sharing a stool, their hands working the same piece of clay. It was their free period, and Mr. Luca never minded if students wanted to kill time *creating*. So there they were, kissing in the back, getting clay handprints all over each other. I went into the art supply room. Henry was already there.

"They'll be gone next year," we said to cheer ourselves up.

"But they'll probably be together forever," Henry said. "Because isn't it always the couples you want to break up that never do?"

The next week in the middle of class, Henry nodded toward the art supply room, and I met him there.

"We got the pleasure of your brother's company last night at dinner," he said. "He's probably a lovely guy when he doesn't have his eyes and hands all over my sister."

"At least they made it through dinner. Last week they disappeared to be alone before their pizza was done cooking and almost burned down our house."

The business of nodding at each other and meeting in the art supply room to complain about Jonathan and Sutton went on through second semester, too, even after we no longer had ceramics class together and would have to sneak through the classroom unnoticed—which wasn't too hard since the door to the art supply closet was by the classroom entrance. After a while, we rarely brought up Sutton and Jonathan.

"I like being alone with you," he said three days before Sutton and Jonathan's graduation.

I didn't know what to say, so I didn't say anything. I looked at the floor.

"Sorry," he said. "I know I'm your worst nightmare, but—"

"You're not," I said, cutting him off. Though I still couldn't look at him.

"I'm not?"

"Wha— Are you fishing for a compliment or something?"

"Yes, exactly."

"You're sort of . . ." *Great* was the word that kept popping up. Because talking to him came as easily as fighting with him. He was this surprise-person who understood me. It was fantastic. And, *fine*, Henry really was insanely attractive. "Perfect," was what came out, and I was mortified.

"Sort of perfect," he said, testing out the words. "Is that the same as almost perfect?"

I shook my head.

"A little bit perfect?"

I shrugged, then nodded.

"I find that grossly vague. What percentages are we talking here? Like eighty percent perfection? I'd like to think it's above fifty, at least." He smiled, which made me smile, and because of the jumpy, fluttery way I was feeling, I was sure I had turned bright red. I covered my face.

"Fifty percent?"

I shook my head, still not looking at him.

"Excellent. Eighty?"

I pulled my hands away from my face and hit him lightly on the shoulder. I let my hand linger; I couldn't help it.

"No," I said. "I just meant that, to me—" But I cut myself off, shaking my head and smiling, oh God, how I was smiling. I went to hit him again, and he caught my hand.

"In that case, I think you're sort of perfect, too."

That was it. If we'd had walls up before, they were down now, a pile of rubble at our feet. I was falling, and admitting to it, and he was right there in it with me. It was so naive of me to think that surrendering to how much I liked him would be the hardest thing I would ever do.

CHAPTER
TWENTY-FIVE

Henry sees me coming before I ring the doorbell. His front door is just a sheet of glass with a dark wood frame. It's set in far enough, with willowy trees and a bamboo fence blocking it from the street, so I guess it's okay for it to be so exposed.

He doesn't look nervous or racked with guilt at all. He looks . . . *wrinkled*. The T-shirt he's wearing appears to have spent the week at the bottom of his backpack.

"What?" he says, opening the door. His right eyebrow rises as he looks at me.

"Nothing." But I stare pointedly at his shirt until he notices. He seems exasperated that I've chosen to bring this up.

"It's not that bad, is it?"

I don't dignify that with an answer as I step inside and Henry closes the door behind me.

"Sorry, I don't iron my T-shirts. It's a *T-shirt.*"

"Right. That'd be insane. Balling it up and sitting on it first is much better."

"It was in my gym bag."

"So it probably smells great, too."

We pause, both sniffing the air but trying not to show it—or that's what I'm doing, at least.

"Of everything in your closet, you thought, a gym-bag shirt is the way to go," I say.

"It's Saturday, so I haven't given any thought to my clothing, and besides, this one is the softest—" He looks away, mortified.

I reach forward and touch it, and he's right—all the fibers have been worn down and the cotton is left feeling velvety. "It's purely functional, clearly."

"All my clothes are purely functional!"

We're both sort of laughing, quiet bursts of chuckles that almost sound like hiccups. We're both shaking our heads.

Henry shrugs. "It's coming off soon anyway, right?" he jokes. It lightens the mood, breaks the tension. He kisses me just as I open my mouth to retort—*If you say so*—and his hands travel to my waist. My hands find his face, hold him close; then they find his shoulders, and I loop my arms around his neck and run my fingers through his hair. We end up on the couch, tossing away throw pillows to make room. We're smiling—part of this is still so insane; it's *insane* to get exactly what you want—but mostly we're kissing. I let my hands go wherever they please, and he does the same thing. Last time we did this I was a bundle of giggles; everything was ticklish. It's different now, and if I laugh, it's because it's too good and I can't help it.

I'd been positive that if we revisited this part of that night, it would be a sad reminder of how the last time we kissed like this, like we were untouchable, the night turned poisonous, and there was a vicious whirlwind that followed, one that put us on separate sides: of the classroom, of the hallway, of the argument about what to do next. That's what I'd thought it would be like whenever I found myself thinking about him—him, and *this*. But it's the opposite.

I don't know how much time passes: hours that feel like days, that still don't feel like long enough. We find ourselves covered in goose bumps and starving. Henry cranks up the heat, even turns on the gas fireplace, so I'm not cold with bare legs wearing Henry's T-shirt and he can stay shirtless. We sit in front of the glowing flames having a carpet picnic, eating pretzels and cookies and whatever else we were able to find in Henry's pantry, and sipping on pink lemonade, Henry's favorite.

We watch a movie, something with lots of explosions and an easy-to-follow plot. If we get distracted, we won't miss much—and we get distracted a lot. When the movie's over, he switches off the fireplace. I can barely see him; there's just intermittent moonlight gleaming through the sliding glass door and the windows in the kitchen.

"You're staying over, aren't you?" he asks.

I'd forgotten all about home, about anything the glow from the fireplace hadn't touched. "Do you want me to—"

"Yes," he interrupts. "Don't you want to?"

"Yes."

His hand finds mine, and he helps me up. He doesn't bother turning on the lights as he steers me through the dark caverns of his house. When we get to the stairs, he lets me go first. I hesitate, not wanting to be the one leading us to his room.

Henry puts his hands against my lower back. "In case you fall," he explains.

"You're the one with the bad knee."

"You're absolutely right."

I laugh as he wraps both his arms tight around me, stepping up so I'm forced to also.

"If I fall, you're going down with me," he says into my ear.

You have no idea, I think.

CHAPTER TWENTY-SIX

Henry's bed isn't made. It's a bed that's been tossed and turned in—like my bed. The dishevelment makes it all the more inviting.

"I couldn't sleep last night," he explains.

"Me neither."

Once we're both under the covers, he switches off the lamp he turned on when we entered. The slanted window above the bed casts shadows, dark blue over black, and leaves streaks of gray light across the bed. We're on our sides, facing each other. His arm hangs over my hips; his fingers softly tap against my back. I keep my hands curled up in front of my chest.

"Can I tell you something?" Henry asks.

"I don't know." I'm very afraid of what he might say to me right now. Something honest, maybe. Or something so perfect it will still haunt me when the sun comes up.

"Henry?" I say, because he hasn't said anything.

"I've missed you for sixteen months."

"Me too. Henry?"

"Yeah?" His hand has moved to my shoulder. Without realizing it, I've reached out and my hands are around his neck.

I was going to ask him to promise that when we fall asleep, he'll still be here in the morning—that nothing, even the most insignificant details, will be like the last time we fell asleep together. But bringing that up feels like it will push us backward, spit us out in a place that reminds us of all the reasons we shouldn't be here, like this.

Instead, I whisper, "I don't know what I'm doing."

He kisses me firmly—it's a kiss that could hold up a building. And it holds me up, too. "It's okay," he says, moving closer.

The next time we kiss, it's like a waterfall; roaring and everywhere and unstoppable. He slips me out of my shirt, out of everything, and when he moves over me, I keep both my hands around his face, kissing him with all I've got. His hand fumbles across the bed, reaching into the nightstand to retrieve a condom. I'm in the process of slipping him out of everything, too, when suddenly he rolls onto his back.

"Amanda—" His voice cuts off, and he swallows hard. The obvious effect I'm having on him makes me swimmy, despite how abrupt it felt when we stopped. "Do—do you remember what you said to me the last time?"

I freeze, completely shocked that he'd bring up that night.

"I'm sorry," he says. "But do you remember?"

"Yes," I mumble. I do remember, and it's unfortunate. What business did I have talking at all that night? But that's what I did, rattled on and on, saying whatever naive and whimsical thoughts passed through my mind.

Henry shifts so he's lying on his side, letting his feet tangle with mine, and tracing a finger over my forehead to chase away stray hairs.

"You said—"

"Henry—" My hair rustles against the pillow as I shake my head.

"You said, 'Don't be so hasty.'"

His smile is bigger than ever. I have to cover my face in case mine is, too. I'm so embarrassed. Why—*why!*—did I think it'd be okay to say that?

"Well, that's not what I'm saying now."

"Mmm." He nods. And fine, back then, that night, it had been like a flood: months of flirtation and weeks of conversation dancing around the possibility that there was something between us, all leading up to a night of kissing. I'd pulled back and he had, too. *Don't be so hasty*—I was borrowing what I'd perceived to be a British phrase to tease him, but I was also serious. I thought there'd be time to wait for the perfect moment. I thought we'd have a hundred perfect moments.

"I was wrong," I whisper. "I had no idea—"

I shake my head, not wanting to admit the rest—that I had no idea how fast things could change; how easily time could slip through my fingers. I prop myself up on my elbows and look right at him. "I've missed you for sixteen months, too, and I want you now, *posthaste*—"

He lets out a burst of laughter, shaking the mattress. "Careful what you wish for."

"Henry."

And now he gives me his full attention. His hand reaches under the sheet and wraps around my waist, like he's going to pull me closer. He closes his eyes for a second. "I've thought about this a million times," he says.

I'm stunned silent by a cataclysmic combustion of happiness and relief. I can only smile.

His leg bends so his knee is resting over mine. I lie on my back, reaching up and locking my hands around his neck, guiding his lips to mine.

"This is what you want?" he says, breaking away. He sounds more nervous than I've ever heard him. We're pressed together so close I think I can feel his heart pounding away. Maybe it's my own racing heart. Maybe it's both of ours.

"Yes," I manage, cupping his cheek with my hand. "Isn't this what you want?"

I feel him nod against my palm.

Again, it's like last time, except now we don't stop. Time trips over itself, and for a moment I inhabit the girl I was then—so hopeful, too hopeful, so sure all of this would come together for her one day, with him. She thanks me silently for giving her what she wanted, for letting her come back here—letting her go through with it when she won't be surprised by what's going to eventually keep them apart, and she won't be alone the next morning.

CHAPTER
TWENTY-SEVEN

Henry's alarm goes off at six a.m.—it blares Jock Jams' "Get Ready for This." I recognize it from the country club's kickboxing class.

"Are you kidding me?" I yell at the ceiling.

Henry fumbles with the alarm, accidentally causing the volume to skyrocket before he manages to turn it off. He lies back down and we laugh—loudly, because we can, and deliriously, because we're still half-asleep.

We're pressed shoulder to shoulder; his hand finds mine and squeezes.

"Are you okay?" he asks.

"I'm stunned and appalled to learn how you start off your

morning, but I'll be all right."

He laughs quietly. "No, I meant, about last night."

Immediately I think of that poem—"i like my body when it is with your body"—and start to blush, remembering in middle school how Dawn and I used to gasp at the words, so sure it would always be the most seductive thing we'd ever read. But I know better than to start quoting E. E. Cummings, or to even admit to the truth: that last night happened because Henry knows all the darkest parts of my mind, and now he knows every inch of me, too. "I'm fine," is all I say.

"It'll be better the next time."

I roll to my side, so he can't see how flushed I am as I reply, "You promise?"

He kisses the exposed skin between my shoulder and my neck and whispers, "I promise."

It's a few hours later when we actually get out of bed. Henry throws on workout shorts and a T-shirt and goes downstairs to make coffee. I change into a T-shirt and sweatpants Henry gave me—not from his gym bag—and use the bathroom. The spare toothbrushes are right where Henry said they'd be, in the third drawer down. I wonder what will become of my toothbrush when I leave; if he'll keep it somewhere for me, in case I'm ever back; if he'll throw it away, knowing I won't be. I fantasize for a moment, *Maybe I'll never go.* The thought makes me smile like a dimwit.

I catch sight of myself in the mirror as I wash my hands. I

look different. There's something unfamiliar about my expression. Like this girl in front of me hasn't been through anything horrible. She's fresh-faced, with a smile playing on her lips, and her eyes look like they'd have to take a trip around the world to find sadness.

"Coffee?" Henry calls from the kitchen when I come downstairs. I can't get to him quick enough. He smiles, and I'm so embarrassed at our uninhibited delight at seeing each other that I pretend some of my excitement is because of the coffee. *Is this how it's supposed to be? How does anyone accomplish anything once they've found their own little world with someone else?*

"I really need fuel." I grab at the coffee like a fiend. Henry's quick; he moves it out of my reach and takes my extended hand, pulling me toward him until I'm close enough to kiss.

"It's equal parts coffee and vanilla cream," he says, inching away slowly and handing me the mug.

I hum with delight as I move to the other side of the kitchen island and take a sip, propping myself up on one of the stools. Henry makes a face, probably because this coffee-cream combination is disgusting to 99 percent of the population.

Henry plays me the message his mother left early this morning that says they're planning to stay another day in Madison and won't be home until Monday.

"I can't stay tonight." Last night, I told my parents I was going out with Graham, but I think even they might start to get suspicious if I don't come home for two days.

"Sure you can."

And I start to think that maybe I really could. It's effortless to pretend I have no one to answer to, and easy to forget I could possibly be hurting anyone, while I'm this happy.

We lounge around flipping channels, watching movies, any excuse to be smashed up next to each other on the couch. We make the brownie mix Henry finds in the pantry and eat it all by the spoonful until there isn't any left to bake. We don't ever stop kissing, and clothes come off, but they're so comfortable and warm we put them back on. We play foosball in Henry's basement. The level of lame trash talking that goes on rivals that of our middle school days.

At eight p.m. we're starved and lazy, and we order delivery from Henry's favorite to-go restaurant. He's offended I've never had their fish-and-chips. We sit in front of the fireplace while we eat it, another carpet picnic. It's so good, and we're so hungry, we moan at the first few bites.

All of a sudden, Henry's eyes go wide.

"What?"

But then I hear for myself—there's a faint noise starting up in the distance, a low humming. The sound of a garage door closing. And soon, the unmistakable click of a door unlocking and people talking in British accents. I have the urge to hide, though I have no idea where. Maybe bolting out the front door is the best option, since the Cranes are coming in through the garage. I look at Henry for a clue.

His face is paling, but he whispers, "It'll be fine."

I don't know if he's talking to me or to himself.

The Cranes are speaking over each other as they enter—a sudden circus bursting into our sanctuary. Mr. Crane can't carry all the bags himself. Sutton left her phone in the car. Mrs. Crane can't believe they drove all the way to Wisconsin just to eat meat loaf. Mr. Crane reminds her that it was also to hold a baby. Sutton accuses them of treating *her* like a baby. Mrs. Crane tells Sutton she thinks she should take a nap.

They all go silent when they spot Henry and me sitting there with messy hair, both dressed in Henry's clothes, and a pile of fish-and-chips in front of us on the floor, the fireplace crackling.

"Oh," Mrs. Crane says. Her smile looks forced, but it could also be because she's tired from traveling. "We've got takeout as well." She holds up a white paper bag. A look of surprise flashes across her face, like she can't believe this is what came out of her mouth. Her eyebrows merge in the middle, and it seems that, more than anything else, she is actually quite sad to have walked into this.

"Brilliant." Henry's smile is an imposter, too. "We've been . . . having a lazy Sunday."

"What are you doing here?" Sutton says. She looks around the room, and I watch as her wide eyes return to their usual perturbed squint. Jonathan isn't here, she gets it now. I notice she's using only one of her crutches to brace herself. Her hair is longer, and straighter. And she's in more clothes than I've ever seen her in before—a black velour tracksuit with big brown slippers that look like they could double as boots. The Sutton I remember had milky-white shoulders always exposed; a skirt that always needed to be pulled down. She's not wearing any makeup either. It's the first time I've seen her without black eyeliner and shimmery pink lip gloss. She looks cleaner, younger. Less like someone Jonathan would have noticed.

"Hi, Sutton." My voice sounds strained and weird. It's not like Sutton to let this go without commenting on it, but thankfully she does. "Hi," I say to the rest of the family.

"Well, come on, boy, help me with these bags," Mr. Crane calls out, his back turned as he's already headed out to the garage.

Henry hesitates, glancing at me, before he follows his dad.

"You're more than welcome to join us at the table," Mrs. Crane says. She won't look me in the eye.

Sutton takes a seat and folds her arms over her chest. "Unless you and Henry prefer to be alone."

"Be nice." Mrs. Crane says this through her teeth, in a hushed tone, but I can still hear her.

"I'm always nice."

The last time I had dinner with a family that wasn't mine, I was at Dawn's. I always helped her mom set the table, and even though it's takeout and setting the table only involves opening bags and passing around plates, I still ask, "Can I help?"

I take a step forward, tripping slightly over Henry's sweatpants because they are too long on me.

"No need," Mrs. Crane says. Her smile is pitying now, but genuine. I hate myself for preferring it this way.

I almost wish she would have screamed at us—kicked me out, threatened to ground Henry. If I were someone else—Imogen, maybe—I wonder if she'd be this nice. The way she looks around, eyes darting between me and Sutton and the garage where Henry has disappeared to—I think mostly she's afraid of me. Like I'm a bomb that's sensitive to too much light or heat or movement, and I'll blow up with news about Jonathan all over their dining room if I'm aggravated. I gather the fish-and-chips from off the floor and bring them to the table.

Henry and his father return with the bags. Mr. Crane is talking to Henry like this is just another day, and he nods along, saying, "Right, right," but his eyes find me and they don't let up. I try to read them for clues. I don't know what he expects me to do.

"Please, have a seat," Mrs. Crane says.

I hesitate before I sit, afraid of taking someone's normal seat.

"Right there is fine." Mrs. Crane motions to the chair across from her.

"Next to Henry." Sutton smiles. Her smile hasn't changed at all. It still reminds you that she isn't the uncomfortable one in the situation, and that she could very well make it worse.

I hear Henry's footsteps moving fast up and down the stairs as he drops off the bags. We all sit staring at each other until he returns to the table. He's breathing heavily from rushing with the luggage, his eyes on me, then his mother, then back on me. He gives Mrs. Crane an apologetic smile as he sits down beside me.

"We decided to come home today after all," she says, looking down.

"So sorry we've spoiled your evening," Sutton says to Henry.

"While the cat's away, indeed," Mr. Crane says, taking a seat and nodding at Henry and me. He laughs. He *actually* laughs. It's the first time I've ever seen Henry's dad. He looks more like Sutton than Henry—pale, with full lips and pragmatic eyes. The way Mr. Crane is smiling, I don't think he knows who I am. He's looking at me like I'm just some girl he caught in his family room with his teenage son.

"At least you didn't burn the house down," he says, serving himself a heaping spoonful of chow mein. "And I guess I don't need to ask you how your weekend was."

Henry keeps his head down as he divvies out the fish-and-chips between us. Eating anything right now seems impossible.

"What happened to Imogen?" Sutton asks. She's sitting at the head of the table, one leg outstretched and braced on a chair that's been pulled up next to her.

"Sutton—" Mrs. Crane hisses.

Mr. Crane covers his mouth.

Sutton sighs like she's bored, picks up an egg roll, and sets it down without taking a bite. "How are you doing, Amanda? How's your family now that the prodigal son has returned?"

"Okay, enough," Henry says quietly.

"I hope everyone's well," Mrs. Crane chimes in softly. She's still smiling, but she's also warning me with her eyes.

I nod, stuffing a bite of fish in my mouth as an excuse to stay silent.

"I've had the absolute worst time trying to get in touch with him," Sutton says. "Not like I can just drive myself over."

Mr. Crane's eyes shift from Henry to me, and I think he's starting to finally understand who I am. A glance at Mrs. Crane, who's looking down at her plate and batting noodles back and forth, confirms it for him.

I'm about to say my line about Jonathan not participating in telecommunications, when Henry saves me.

"Don't, Sutton."

Sutton ignores him. "Amanda, darling, when you get home, tell your brother to call me straightaway. I have the most alarming bit of gossip to share." She turns her attention to Henry, and her smile widens.

If this were an exchange in the hallway at Garfield High, now would be the time I'd say, "What do you want?" And whatever it was, I'd give it to her.

"We talked about this, Sutton," Mrs. Crane says.

"Remember what Dr. Allister said," Mr. Crane adds. His expression is so stern, I can hardly remember the jolly jokester he'd seemed like just seconds ago.

"You all have to stop," she says. "Relax, okay? You know the reason I have to get in touch with him. It's what they want! It's what she would have wanted, too!" Sutton raises her arm and motions in my direction.

At first I think she's pointing at me. But when Mr. Crane follows his daughter's finger, his eyes are fixed above me. I glance over my shoulder and see it. A large framed photograph of Grace and Sutton. They're smiling and standing arm in arm on my porch as the sun beams down around them. Jonathan was there, I think. Maybe he was the one who took the picture.

Henry puts his hand on the back of my chair, but only for a moment.

"Henry?" Sutton says, her eyes still crazed with fury. "Since you're apparently very close with Amanda, did you tell her why I need to talk to Jonathan now that he's . . . available?" There's a small quiver in her lips. I've never seen her look or act this desperate. Her stare is like venom.

"The Marlamounts want to talk to him—to us," she explains. "They don't want another apology or anything, but like it or not, he was one of the people who knew Grace best." She sniffles, tears welling slowly behind her eyes. "They only want to sit down—with both of us—and talk about her. They just want to hear more about what she was like from her best friends."

Sutton looks around the table, like she's examining everyone's reaction. Her eyes are locked on me when she finally says, "So think about it."

She pushes her chair out from the table, and the crutch that was balanced against the back of the chair falls to the floor. Henry gets up and retrieves it for her. He offers her his hand, too, but she doesn't take it. We're all quiet as she holds on to the table to lift herself up, takes her crutch from Henry, and limps away.

"I should go," I say, standing up, anxious to get out of here, too. Henry's mother nods, staring at her plate, and I feel more hurt by this one small action than I could have imagined.

I turn to Henry. I whisper, "I just have to—" I clumsily gesture to the shirt I'm wearing. *His shirt.*

I hear Henry apologizing to his parents as I pick my clothes up off the family room floor and disappear into the closest bathroom to change as fast as I possibly can.

Henry's right outside the door when I open it. He takes his balled-up clothes from me and tosses them into the laundry room across the hall.

We don't talk as I follow him to the front door. I don't look at him, and I'm pretty sure he's not looking at me either.

CHAPTER
TWENTY-EIGHT

Henry still hasn't said anything by the time we reach the end of the walkway outside, so I start talking. "Do you want me to tell him to call her? Do they need to meet with—"

"No," Henry says. "It's an excuse. We're in touch with the Marlamounts. They can talk to Sutton about Grace whenever they want—which they never do, because Sutton is so unstable. If they wanted to talk to Jonathan, they wouldn't go about it through her."

"Okay."

"I'm sorry you had to see her like that." He's talking more to the ground than to me, and when he does look at me, his gaze is fixed on my right ear, my chin, my shoulder, but never my eyes.

He's visibly uncomfortable, just like his mother was—it makes me feel as though I'm best forgotten, just like Jonathan.

This is the future we were imagining when we decided to *forget it* way back when. It's caught up to us, and it didn't take long. I think of Graham, and it makes me sick.

"I'll see you at school, okay?"

"What—wait," he says, shaking his head. "Wait."

I don't blame him for not saying anything else, for staring at me like for once he's the one who's sorry.

"It's all right," I tell him. "It's . . . it is what it is." I use Jonathan's line because it's the only one that seems to fit. "We don't have to talk about last night. We don't need to dissect what it means, or what we're supposed to do about it."

"I already know what it means." He looks to his feet. "What it meant."

I take his use of past tense as a cue to walk away, but he doesn't let me. He's in front of me with one hand on my shoulder and the other on my hip.

"Wait," he says again, and again he doesn't have any more words, so I'm the one who speaks.

"Is *this* what you want, Henry?" My voice cracks, and he tightens his grip around my shoulder, as if this is going to help. It makes him feel better, I guess. He thinks he's comforting me. He doesn't realize he's just making things harder. "Did you see the way they were looking at us?"

"Shhh. It doesn't matter to me."

"I have to get out of here." It must be what he wants, too,

deep down. He must know what a relief it will be once I'm gone and there's no reason for Sutton's eyes to get large and hopeful over the possibility of getting in touch with someone so toxic. No reason for her to lie to explain why it's a good idea to talk to Jonathan and not just indulgent and desperate on her part. No reason for Henry's dad to stop laughing or for his mother to turn sad.

"I'll go with you," he says.

It makes me want to laugh, cry, sigh—all at the same time. "There's nowhere for us to go."

"Sure there is." He leans in so our noses touch, then our foreheads.

That's all that's left of the weekend—of Henry and me—impossible suggestions, inevitable good-byes.

I lean away from him, and his grip on me tightens.

"Don't," he says.

"Henry—"

"I know what you're about to say, and just, *don't*."

"One of us has to say it." I raise my voice and it splinters. "We don't work so well outside of your empty house."

"Why?" he says. "Because of other people? Other people, who don't matter?"

I gesture to his house, letting my hand fall limp against my side. To drive the point home, I add, "Graham? Imogen?"

"You know what I mean."

I take a deep breath to conjure some courage. "What about Jonathan?"

Henry lets go of me, and it feels like he's dropped me.

Jonathan—what's been silencing his voice every time he's told me to *wait* since we've been out here.

"What about him?" Henry spits the words.

But it's all about my brother: what he did, what he's done since then. How all of us are collateral in the fallout. Henry knows—and I can tell he does because of his clenched fists and his new frown—that there will never be common ground for us on this issue. There isn't supposed to be. It doesn't matter. It's useless because we can't change the past and we can't change how we feel. Henry wants Sutton to forget about Jonathan. I want Jonathan to be someone Sutton doesn't have to forget.

"Your family thinks of him when they look at me. Everyone does." Gone are the days when this was a good thing.

"That's not what I see."

"That's what you try not to see."

"Fine," he says, throwing his hands up in surrender. "But it doesn't change that I care about you."

Maybe his feelings for me and mine for him should conquer everything else—Graham, Imogen, Henry's parents, their anger at Jonathan, my parents and their strained hope for Jonathan, Sutton's denial, her unresolved grief, Jonathan's selfishness. What a world that would be. But it's not the one we're living in.

"Henry, it's not enough." I take his hands as I say it.

His shoulders fall, like he's tired of arguing, or too hurt to continue. Most likely, it's that he knows I'm right and fighting anymore is pointless.

"I don't think we should tell anyone," I say.

He hesitates, but then, he nods.

"I wouldn't change last night," I say as tears burn my eyes, "but—I just—I don't know how to *be* after that. You know—"

"It's okay," he says. "It's okay," he repeats in a whisper. He moves to wipe under his eye with the back of his hand and takes my hand along for the ride.

"I don't want to be someone you feel like you have to apologize to, or someone you don't think you should cry in front of—" He breaks off, shaking his head.

"You're not." It's an easy promise; it's the truth.

"All right," he whispers, staring down at our hands. I give them a final squeeze, and when I let go, he lets go, too.

CHAPTER
TWENTY-NINE

*S*aying good-bye at Grace's funeral was overwhelming.

So I didn't do it.

I took one look at that full church, the coffin in front, the flowers swallowing the altar, the blown-up photo of Grace at age sixteen, the oldest she would ever be, and knew this was the saddest and scariest place I would ever set foot.

Sutton Crane was the final straw, the real reason I left the church. She sat in the first row, in the aisle, since her back had to be at a certain angle and both her legs were wrapped in casts and had to be kept straight, so she didn't fit in the rows reserved for wheelchairs. She was crying without sobbing. Her stare was vacant and tears ran steadily down her cheeks in black lines, carrying her eyeliner to her chin and staining the top of her neck brace. It looked like she'd died, too.

I was afraid that if she saw me, her eyes would spring to life in search of Jonathan, who wasn't coming.

Henry never told me what had chased him outside, but there we were, standing next to a stained-glass window on what otherwise would have been a lovely summer day, while the funeral went on without us.

"Is he here?" Henry asked. We hadn't spoken in three weeks. We hadn't even tried. The funeral had been delayed because of the media frenzy that followed the accident, and even with the extra time, I still had no idea what to say to him.

I shook my head.

"Do you want to talk about what happened, you know, with us?" Henry said, his voice lifeless.

"No," I said, without hesitation.

He ran his hands through his hair, tugging on the ends—and then did it again and again and again. If he did want to talk about it, he didn't know how.

"Let's just forget it," Henry said, and I felt ten thousand pounds being lifted off my chest. We were kissing while Grace was dying. I wanted to forget everything about that night. I think that's how he must've felt, too. He took a huge breath, like maybe it was the first one he'd taken in three weeks.

I agreed with a nod, and made it official by being the first to walk away.

CHAPTER
THIRTY

I've pulled onto the road and am about to shift from reverse to drive. Henry's there suddenly, out of breath and knocking on my window.

I put the car in park but don't turn off the engine. My heart is beating a million times a minute as I open the door, climbing out of the car to tell him I made a mistake and I don't think we should forget it either.

But Henry's expression is still sullen. He's out of breath from running, not from the all-consuming desire to sweep me off my feet and carry me back up to his bedroom, parents be damned.

"You forgot your phone," he says, holding it out.

"Thanks." The letdown is obvious in my voice.

We both just stand there, and I'm wondering why he hasn't moved yet, when he bites down on the corner of his lip.

"Actually, you didn't really forget your phone," he says. "It was lifted from your purse."

He steps back, shrugging, shaking his head. And he's gone without offering more of an explanation. It's not necessary anyway.

I know exactly who took my phone, and what she used it for.

CHAPTER
THIRTY-ONE

The outgoing calls list on my phone has just one new entry since being liberated from my bag. A call to Jonathan. A call that was answered. A call that lasted forty-eight seconds.

I don't know how much damage could've been done in forty-eight seconds.

There's an unfamiliar car parked in front of our house. A green Jeep that I've never seen before. I try calling Dawn twice between parking and walking into the house—stalling going inside and seeing my brother. I need her advice so I can deal with whatever's waiting for me at home. Both calls go straight to voice mail.

"There she is," Jonathan singsongs as I walk in the door. He's sitting in the living room with Wren. He's in his favorite recliner. She's got her shoes off and is curled up on the couch wearing one of Jonathan's sweatshirts, with her legs tucked under a blanket. She's leaning as close to the recliner as she can get. They both hold mugs. I don't even kid myself into thinking it's hot chocolate in their cups.

"Where are Mom and Dad?"

Jonathan points to the ceiling. Upstairs. Nestled in bed, and that single missed call I have from Standard Dad this afternoon was simply a courtesy, I guess.

"What are you guys doing?" I ask.

"Just hanging," Jonathan says.

Wren has on an insane smile, and her cheeks are flushed.

There's a dip in Jonathan's neck, a laziness to his smile, a mischievous glower to his eyes. He's drunk. Or on his way there.

"Can I talk to you a second, in private?" I say to Jonathan.

"Whatever you want to say to me, you can say in front of her."

I stare at him, waiting for it to hit him that there are many things I could possibly say right now that he wouldn't want Wren to hear.

"Out with it." He motions with his hand like I'm about to physically give him something.

"I don't think you should be drinking," I say, instead of asking him about Sutton. "What if your probation officer—"

"Who, Gary?"

"That'd be him."

"Naw, Gary and I are cool."

"Jonathan—" But has he forgotten? He meets with Gary once a week, and Gary can choose to drug-test at every meeting if he wants.

"I said, it's *cool*." He stands up and looks me right in the eyes, like this is going to convince me.

He's too determined, so I just shrug. "Whatever you say. It's your jail cell."

"Ouch. Below the belt, baby sister." He steps back, grabbing his heart, and falls next to Wren on the couch. Watching her smile, he scoots closer and props his head up on her shoulder. There's a second when he looks at her and he seems just as entranced as she does. He's going to kiss her, I think. She thinks it too, and slightly tilts her head in his direction.

I'm about to say something to stop it—maybe now *would* be the perfect time to bring up Sutton—but Jonathan speaks first. "Are you tired?" he asks Wren.

"No," she says, her voice sultry.

I clear my throat, to remind them that I'm here, though that's never stopped my brother from flirting shamelessly in front of me before.

"Good." Jonathan stands. He holds his hand out to her. "Then it's the perfect time to go to bed."

Great.

I step forward and grab his hand before Wren can. "One second," I tell her. I pull Jonathan around the corner into the kitchen. He lets me drag him.

"That was rude." He looks like he wants to burst out laughing. "And you're in trouble, *young lady*." He wags his finger in my face. "Standard Dad was asking about you—where you were, and why you hadn't come home. I told him to calm down, you were fine—you're welcome."

"I was—" I decide to cut to the chase. "Sutton got ahold of my phone and—"

"Oh, I *know*." He laughs.

"What'd she say?"

My brother is still smiling—too happily, I think, for having been ambushed by the ex-girlfriend he was intent on avoiding. "I'm not even going to ask how she got your phone—or why you were gone all night and all day and obviously not at Graham Sicily's."

I open my mouth, hoping a reasonable excuse will magically fall out.

"Shh, shhh—I don't want to know what you were doing at Sutton's." He closes his eyes, plugs his ears. I pull on his arm until he drops his hands and opens his eyes.

"What is Wren doing over here?" I say, bringing this conversation back where it belongs.

"She brought the beverages."

"So I smell."

"And she's beautiful, you know." His eyes have softened, and it makes him look inarguably sincere.

"What are you thinking?" I'm pleading with him. He's got to see what's wrong with this picture—that this girl who worships him for all the wrong reasons and who brings whiskey right to his doorstep when he's risking so much just by taking a sip isn't someone he should be inviting into his life, or his bedroom. I wish I'd never taken him to that damned Starbucks.

"The answer to that hasn't changed: I'm not." He cheerily sings the last two words as he walks away.

I know I should let him go, but I follow him around the corner.

Wren is standing at the bottom of the stairs, holding her shoes in her hand, waiting for him. He offers her his arm.

"Good night," I call to their backs as they stroll up the stairs. They don't even turn around.

"Jonathan," I shout, reaching for something to say that will make him feel bad or punish him for being so indiscreet and, at the same time, so much like the person he used to be. The two of them disappear into his room before I can think of anything.

I don't hear them the entire night; I never did when Jonathan had "guests"—mostly Sutton—stay over. Our house is perfectly designed for privacy, with closets and bathrooms and guest rooms acting as barriers between our bedrooms. Not a sound gets through. Standard Dad and Mumsy will sleep peacefully in their bedroom at the far end of the hall, completely clueless, just like in the old days.

Wren's gone in the morning. So is Jonathan.

Something incredible happened with Henry
[Deleted, 12:13 a.m.]

So I've never felt like this before, and I probably sound crazy
[Deleted, 12:13 a.m.]

You're going to tell me I made a giant mistake, and I know I did, but
[Deleted, 12:14 a.m.]

I'm never going to be able to sleep again, because every time I close my eyes
[Deleted, 12:14 a.m.]

There are some things you can never forget even if you should, and Henry
[Deleted, 12:14 a.m.]

I missed him for sixteen months, but it wasn't like this—
[Deleted, 12:14 a.m.]

If you don't hear from me after tonight, it's because I've ripped my brain from my skull to stop thinking about
[Deleted, 12:15 a.m.]

I wish everything was different
[Deleted, 12:17 a.m.]

I hope you and Becky had a great time in L.A. over the weekend. I'm sure you saw, and made out with, lots of movie stars. Can't wait for a recap.
[Sent, 12:20 a.m.]

CHAPTER
THIRTY-TWO

On Monday in sixth period, Henry's by the door, I'm by the window.

I'm still with Graham, and Henry's still with Imogen. All that's really new is that it's harder to look at him and not remember us in his room Saturday night. So I try very hard not to look at him at all. This is, of course, impossible.

On Tuesday I see him shuffling down the hall with his head bowed, scratching the back of his neck, and right when he seems like he's about to look up and will see me coming his way, my whole body seizes up. I duck into the bathroom and close myself in a stall, hyperventilating so badly that someone knocks on the stall door to ask if I'm okay. I practically scream at her, "I'm fine!" though I hadn't meant to yell.

Once I've calmed down a little, I call Dawn. She's the only one who'll be able to talk me through this. I have to tell her.

"Hello?" When she answers, her voice is radiant, and I can hear Becky cackling in the background. I opt for asking about L.A. instead, and strain to pay attention as Dawn puts the phone on speaker and she and Becky give me a rundown. Sometimes they're laughing so hard I can hardly understand what they're saying. When she asks what's new with me, I tell them about Jonathan and Wren.

"She's just bad for him, you know?" I say.

"A bad girl for a bad boy." Becky makes a joke, and Dawn actually laughs.

"You shouldn't be surprised that he's hooking up with some-one, Amanda," Dawn says to my silence.

I know she's right.

But I still find myself wondering about Wren, about them. Every day, he sees her. He goes for his run before I come down-stairs to make breakfast. Maybe there's more to it than Jonathan making the most of his fifteen minutes of fame and capitalizing on sex and whiskey delivery. On Wednesday, he doesn't get back until after two p.m., jogging up the driveway right as I'm getting home.

"Do you just hang out there like a creepy stalker while she works?" I ask him in the kitchen that evening. Jonathan's making a salad. Mumsy and Standard Dad are out to dinner with some friends from the club.

"She wasn't working today," he says.

"You smell like cigarettes." I tried to insult him about this earlier by hacking loudly when he walked past. He pretended not to notice.

"Off the wagon. I decided to indulge. But I went for a run, and I'm having salad for dinner." He throws the tomatoes in with bravado. "It balances."

"If you say so."

His grin reassures me that he's joking—he doesn't really think a salad cancels out a cigarette.

Thursday evening, there's a lightness to him. He seems filled with energy in a walking-on-air sort of way. He's in the den watching television when I get back from Graham's, where I went after school.

"Did you have fun with your beau?" he asks. He rolls his eyes.

Mumsy is in her room, best guess. My father sits at the dining room table with his laptop open in front of him, sipping on tea and holding his forehead.

"Have you had dinner yet?" I ask Jonathan.

He shakes his head.

"Want to get out of here?" I twirl my car keys on my fingers.

"How can I refuse?"

We walk to the entry and get our coats.

"Where are you going?" Standard Dad says. He sounds

exhausted by the idea of having to ask us.

"We'll be right back," I say, realizing this might mean nothing coming from me, since I failed to come home on Saturday night and all day Sunday, though no one has confronted me about it. "We're just going to Hal's Diner."

He stands, and I think he might want us to invite him. But he can't relax around Jonathan, and Jonathan can't relax around him. We say good-bye and don't wait for him to say good-bye back.

CHAPTER
THIRTY-THREE

Jonathan orders us both chocolate shakes and cheeseburgers. This is the kind of place our parents would never go, which is why Jonathan and I used to come here all the time, starting the second he got his license and we finally had the freedom to go anywhere. Grace once made a March Madness–style score sheet for everything on the one-page laminated menu, pitting the mashed potatoes against the steak fries, the veggie burger against the tuna melt. The big winner was the cheeseburger.

"I guess today you'll be giving up cigarettes for grease," I say. "*Balance*, right?"

He winks. "And here I thought you brought me to the diner to harass me about Wren. And my 'drinking.'" He makes the air quotes symbol with his fingers as he says this.

"Nope." I hold my up hands. "Honestly, I don't want to know." I mimic him from Sunday night, plugging his ears, closing his eyes. I didn't bring him here to talk about Wren.

"Sutton, then?" he asks. He shakes his head at the same time that I do, but for an entirely different reason. "I can see it in your face—you have an agenda."

"Me? Never."

He drums his fingers on the table, considering, then says, "Actually, I have something to ask you."

I let out a big, exasperated sigh, in case he's going to ask about last weekend.

He doesn't react to this. "Are you okay?" he says. He pouts slightly, the way he does unconsciously sometimes when he's talking to our mom and thinks she needs comforting.

"Of course," I tell him. I'm putting everything I have into sounding confident, but still it comes out lacking.

"Are you sure?" There's nothing in his voice but sincerity. One hundred percent my brother, just wondering, just checking. The way he used to.

He asks again, and that's all it takes to summon my tears. I blink them away, but he reaches across the table and grabs my hand. He can be so sweet sometimes. It makes me feel bad now, for what I'm about to do. But I have to. He has to purge, so he'll stop bingeing—on Wren, on alcohol, on his own anger. The root of all his issues lies with one person.

"Tell me about Grace," I say as the waitress sets the food in front of us. Jonathan smiles at her, and for a moment I think he hasn't heard me. But then she leaves and he speaks.

"As if my words could do her justice." He takes a huge bite of his cheeseburger.

"Jonathan."

"Nothing could do her justice," he says with his mouth full.

I wait for him to look at me. He doesn't want to, and when his eyes finally shift to mine, I see why. He's about to cry. I've never seen him do it before, not since we were very little and crying was inspired only by physical injuries and minor disappointments. In the aftermath of Grace's death he had bloodshot eyes, leftover sniffles, an unmoving frown. But no tears.

"What am I supposed to say?" It comes out as a whisper, though I don't think he meant it to. His mouth seems thick with saliva, and more tears fill his eyes in a sudden surge.

"Say anything," I whisper back. "Say everything." I'm going to cry, too, any second now.

He wipes at a drip under his nose and looks away.

"I don't deserve to talk about her. Didn't deserve to know her." He sniffles. "And she definitely didn't deserve me." A single tear snakes out. Jonathan closes his eyes, like that's going to stop the rest of them. "I don't want to talk about it."

"But you went on that show," I say.

"It was a lapse in judgment."

"Give me the real reason, Jonathan."

He stares dully at me, his expression returning to normal. "Fame. Power. Money." My heart drops.

"Just be serious, for a second."

"Second's up."

"You should be able to talk to me—I'm your . . . It's *us*, Jonathan." As I'm thinking about the way we used to be, a few tears escape. "Talk to me about her, just let yourself go through whatever you have to go through, this way, the right way, not—"

"Oh." And he laughs, but it's cruel. "So that's what this is about? This is you playing AA, making me talk about my feelings. You think I need help."

"Don't you? Isn't that why you're still drinking, even now, when the consequences are—"

He laughs again, his eyes rolling slightly. "Don't talk to me about consequences," he mumbles.

"You keep getting worse." The words are out of my mouth before I can think better of them, but I don't care.

"How could I possibly get any worse?" he says, with a taunting chuckle. He takes another enormous bite.

I'm sitting here in tears; he's wearing a grin. I'm nauseous, he's gorging—unaffected and making a point of it. But why? *Why?*

"I can't stand this," I say.

Jonathan tilts his head in a mockingly sympathetic way. "There are very few things you can stand, baby sister."

"What's that supposed to mean?"

"Nothing, forget what I said—"

"No, what did you mean by that, Jonathan? Tell me."

"You're closed off; that's all I meant."

There's a stinging in my chest as he continues.

"You're very selective about who you let in, and once you accept someone, you want them to be a certain way, no matter what. That explains why you're dating a boring, shallow guy like Graham—even while you're spending your time . . . elsewhere. And I *am* messed up, baby sister, look at me. This is what I am now, and there's no changing it."

If honesty is a weapon, Jonathan wields it like a pro. The truth hurts the worst. My tears are resurfacing. My nose wants to run, but I do not want to sniffle right now. I don't want him to know the effect he has.

"Don't use my 'closed-off' disposition as the reason why I think you need help."

He pulls a napkin out of the dispenser and holds it out to me. "You miss Dawn a lot, huh?"

Changing the subject is not going to work with me. "*Jonathan*. Stop it."

"You telling me not to be fucked up after what I've been through is like me telling you not to miss Dawn."

I snatch the napkin from him and mop up the tears that are escaping. Half of them are tears of anger.

"I actually love your *disposition*," he says, pulling more napkins for me. "I'll never think anyone's good enough for you. It's comforting knowing you aren't going to let just anybody in."

It's no use. I reach for my own napkins now.

"I'm not trying to change you, Jonathan; I'm trying to help you. There is such a thing as healing."

He brushes off his hands, still seemingly unmoved by anything I've said, or by my tears. "You know what people are always telling me?" He crosses his arms, resting his elbows on the edge of the table.

I shake my head.

"'You're so lucky to be alive.'"

I lean back into the booth. This is the thought I don't allow myself to have, ever. How lucky he is—how lucky I am—that he's alive. This is the part of that night I keep buried the deepest—the part I wish I could forget. Because the moment I found out what happened, I felt relief. My brother was still alive.

"I don't really know what to do with that, you know?" He picks up what's left of his cheeseburger. "On one hand, it's like, here's the perfect second chance to live right, be healthy. Eat well, exercise—use my legs because I'm so lucky to have use of them." He keeps a straight face as he says this. I don't know how.

"Get a good job. Find a respectable girl. Be honorable." He shrugs. "But is that really living at all?"

I watch as he polishes off his cheeseburger and licks his fingers clean. "What would Grace say?" I ask.

"We'll never know, will we?" he says, still impassive.

My jaw drops open.

"Whatever is wrong with you—whatever you think you've become—it doesn't justify how selfish and reckless and nasty you're being." I rush out of the restaurant, leaving behind an untouched milk shake and a full plate. I jump in the car, start the engine, and pinch my eyes shut, imagining what it would be like to take off down the road, leaving him stranded at the diner the way I want to. I think of Henry, and all my caged feelings break free. I start to cry.

Jonathan takes his time before he comes back to the car. "It's going to be okay, Amanda."

I turn up the radio so it's too loud for me to hear if he says anything else on our way home.

CHAPTER
THIRTY-FOUR

The memories I have of Grace are small.

I remember the cartwheel races we used to have at Stony Day Elementary—upside-down memories of her focused eyes, her hand against the grass, her legs soaring through the air. When she was part of my group for the eighth-grade egg-drop contest, it was her idea to draw a face on the egg complete with long lashes, red lips, and a mole like Marilyn Monroe's. The last year she was alive, she used to spin around to look at me whenever our world history teacher made jokes about there being a lot of knights during the Dark Ages, because she knew it was exactly the type of thing that I'd find amusing.

I remember her ringtone. Lady Gaga's "Poker Face." And

that her favorite movie when we were little was *The Wizard of Oz*. She had a pair of ruby slippers. I remember the way she used to touch things when she walked by them—her fingers beating against chain-link fences, her hand running over closed lockers, her knuckles rapping on the hoods of cars. Like seeing the world was just not enough.

It's important she was happy before she left us. I want to know what she and Jonathan had been laughing about at graduation, what she'd been scolding him about at Sylvia's party. I still think of her here sometimes, witnessing all of this. Twisted, I know, but ironic also, because she might be the only person who could get him through this.

She'd bridge the gap between him and Sutton; she'd tell him to stay far away from Wren; chastise him for drinking while on probation. She'd tell him to give Gary a chance, and he would. She'd tell him that AA couldn't hurt and wouldn't encourage him to do any more speaking engagements, and he'd listen to her. There was something about Grace, for him—I can't pretend to know what it was. But maybe if he remembers it, her magic can still work on him.

That's my wish. That's the only thing I want that doesn't feel like it might be a long shot.

I want him to remember.

CHAPTER
THIRTY-FIVE

This is what a Friday night should be. Graham with his arm around me. The vocal stylings of a band from Indiana ringing through the air, which smells entirely of coffee. I so need this—*fun*—after that awful fight yesterday with Jonathan. I haven't seen him since slamming the door to my room after we got home from the diner. I'm rolling on two mochas; enough caffeine that my foot is tapping faster than the music. I try for a twirl, and Graham laughs.

"Nice moves," he says, pulling me closer.

Jonathan's wrong about us. So we're not like Sutton and him? They were a mess of feelings, a concoction of uncontrollable urges, complicated even more by the fact that Sutton's anger was easily sparked, and Jonathan's talent for igniting it was directly proportional to his flair for flirting with other girls. We're the anti-Jonathan-and-Sutton. Graham is a "lightweight" and I hate anything that tastes like Pine-Sol.

Even if I'm wrapped up in denial about everything I've done to ruin what I have with Graham, I don't care. It's hard to forget the events of last weekend, and I've been so overly nice to Graham, I wonder if he is suspicious. But as far as he knows, I barely talk to anyone else, so even if he suspects something, there's nothing for him to pin his doubt on.

I put my arms around Graham's neck as we dance in the crowd, and when the applause erupts, he leans down and kisses me, quickly. But perfectly.

I could do *this* all day and all night—kissing, dancing, laughing. The only reason I stop is because my phone starts to ring. The name on the screen makes my head swirl. *Standard Dad's cell.* I haven't seen him since last night either.

Graham sees the screen and nods toward the front door, telling me to take it outside where it's probably quieter. But the sidewalk outside the coffee shop looks just as crowded as the inside—and just as loud. I move toward the back, down the hallway, thinking the bathroom will be a better solution, but of course there's a line. The door at the end of the hallway is marked EXIT, so I push through it.

By the time I'm in the back lot, next to the Dumpsters, my phone is no longer ringing. I'm about to call him back when my phone beeps, signaling a new voice message.

I pace back and forth as I listen to my dad's voice, intelligible but still muffled by background noise on his end. "Hey, Amanda, it's Dad. I was hoping you could swing by and pick me up from Newton's. I just think . . . it's a better idea for me to get a ride. The cab company said it'd be an hour wait. That's insane, right? Anyway, sorry to interrupt your night, sweetheart. I don't mind waiting for a cab, if you're busy."

It's unlike any message I've ever received. From anyone. But especially my dad. I've never heard his voice trying so hard to be upbeat, and failing so miserably. I never know what my dad is up to on a Friday night, but I never assumed it was drinking alone at Newton's, a dive bar by the overpass. I cover my mouth, frozen and staring at my phone like any second there'll be another message: "Just kidding! Everything is fine."

I look up because I hear footsteps. Henry appears from behind the Dumpster.

"What are you—" I don't finish because Henry's buttoning his pants, refastening his belt.

"I'm not proud of it, but have you seen the line for the bathroom?"

"And coffee is a natural diuretic." I'm relieved to see him; relieved to be speaking to him. But I feel like I'm going to burst out laughing—crazed, manic laughter—because here *he* is, smiling, and looking just as relieved to see me. A mere five minutes ago I had convinced myself that I could forget my feelings for him, but now that he's here in front of me, they've detonated and are exploding all over the place.

"Is that the reason you're back here, too?" he says.

Some of the bottled-up laughter escapes, and we stand there for a second, laughing together like we really are crazy. Before I can wrap my head around it, before I can even pose the question, *What are we doing?*, my phone starts ringing again. I answer it with a trembling hand.

"Hi, Dad," I say, pressing my phone against my ear and turning away from Henry. "I can come get you."

"Okay, thanks." He sounds like himself, though the background is noisy. "Do you know where to go?"

"Yeah. I'll be there soon." I hang up before he thanks me again. "Shit," I say, running my hand over my eyes as if this will make it easier to focus. This is such a mess. What am I supposed to say to Graham? I don't want him to know; I don't want to watch his expression turn sympathetic, don't want to hear him tell me it's okay when it's not, it's so obviously not. He'll rest his hands on my shoulders, and I'll be able to see in his eyes that he's thinking about my brother—*this is what Jonathan should have done.*

It should be so easy to think of an excuse for why I need to be taken home right this second—but I can't concentrate. My thoughts keep coming back to the image of my father in his starched and creased button-down shirt, with his clean-shaven face and graying eyebrows, sitting alone, throwing back so much whiskey he has to call his seventeen-year-old daughter to pick him up. Standard Dad wrecked. I don't want to see him like that.

"Amanda?" *Amander.*

"Can you—I need—" It feels like so much effort to ask this, to admit to this. Henry steps closer. I focus on his foot. The way his shoe makes a crunching noise as it hits the dirty pavement.

"I need a ride home," I manage.

"Let's go," is all he says.

I follow him around the side of the building to his car.

I mean to say thank you, but my mind is a frenzy of worry over what I'm going to find at Newton's, and how I'm going to explain my disappearance to Graham.

As soon as we're on the road, Henry asks, "Do you want to tell me what's going on?"

I spill everything. Once I start talking, it's easy to keep going.

Henry nods along. He doesn't say anything until I've gotten it all out. "Okay." His voice is steady and calm. "I'll take you to Newton's. If your dad's car is there, you can drive it back. If it's not, I'll take you both home."

I close my eyes. I hate the possibility of Henry being around for whatever transpires after my father comes out of Newton's. But I find myself saying, "Okay," and feeling tremendous relief.

"And here's what to say to Graham."

"What?"

"Type this, verbatim: 'My mother called to say she was out-side waiting for me—needs me home straightaway. I'll call you tomorrow.'"

I do as he says, switching out "straightaway" for "right away," editing out the British, and press send. Just a few seconds later my phone beeps.

"Shit."

"What's it say?" Henry asks.

I read the text out loud. "'Is everything all right? Do you need anything? What happened?'"

"Tell him everything's fine and your mum just needed you to help her with some last-minute stuff that she couldn't get done on her own tonight."

I'm typing everything he says, substituting "mother" for "mum." It sounds like something that Graham will believe.

Graham responds in seconds. I don't wait for Henry to ask before I read him the latest text. "'Ellen said she saw you leaving in Henry Crane's car. What's really going on?'"

"Tell him to bugger off," Henry mutters.

"I'll just tell him the truth." I bend my legs up so I can lay my head against my knees.

"It's none of his business, Amanda," Henry says. "It doesn't have to be."

I don't say anything else, and neither does he. I turn my phone off, and the rest of the ride is completely silent.

CHAPTER
THIRTY-SIX

My dad is waiting outside Newton's when we pull up. He's standing next to his car, leaning against the passenger door with his arms crossed in front of him, staring at the ground.

"Thank you," I tell Henry.

"Of course," he says.

Henry drives toward the parking lot exit but doesn't leave. He parks on the other side of the lot. Probably so my dad won't see him.

My dad doesn't notice me until I'm approaching him. I hope my hey-how's-it-going smile doesn't look as painful and misplaced as the one he's giving me when he passes me his keys.

"Thanks, Amanda."

I thought that maybe he'd have trouble walking. Maybe his eyes would be heavy the way Jonathan's eyes always get when he's drinking. Maybe his words would run together. But he doesn't appear to be drunk at all.

We're quiet at first. Just the low hum of talk radio in the background as we cruise down the road. Henry trails behind us but turns left when we get to the second light.

"Sorry you had to take time out of your Friday night to come get me," he says. He's trying so hard to sound positive.

"Dad?"

"Yeah?"

"You don't even seem drunk." I think it might make him feel better. Less ashamed, maybe.

He chuckles, quickly and quietly. "I don't know that I really am drunk."

I look at him. His eyes are glassy, and he sniffles, like he might be about to cry. My instinct is to get out of the car and run away, ditch him and the car right here in the middle of the intersection. If he really does cry, I won't be able to handle it.

"I had a whiskey and some beers," he tells me.

This isn't a surprise. When my father drinks, he has either a couple of glasses of red wine, or a whiskey and a few beers. This is what he always drinks when we go out to eat. He's never asked someone else to drive.

"I'm probably fine," my father says. "But I don't know . . ."

I nod, grateful I have to watch the road so I don't have to look at my dad. I know all too well what's been eating at him—the lingering and constant thought waving from miles ahead: one false move and things can go all wrong. One false move and you can ruin things for yourself, and for other people, too.

He clears his throat. "If you ever need a ride, for any reason, at any time, call me and I'll come get you. I won't ask questions. I won't be angry. You won't get in trouble. Just, if you can't drive, call me, and I'll gladly pick you up." It's so cliché, so Standard Dad, I'm surprised he's never said it before—even after the accident.

"Okay," I answer quickly.

"You know that, right? That you can always call me?"

I'm nodding. But it's a lie. If I were ever in trouble, where I needed a ride, I would call a cab. I probably would've even waited an hour for its arrival.

"I'm sorry I didn't say it sooner," he says. The leather squeaks as he shifts in his seat. "I just . . . I thought it was something you already knew."

I speed up when we get to the last stoplight before we reach our house. The longer we're in this car together, the more time he has to confess that he never made this offer to Jonathan. And then I'll have to reassure him that what happened that night wasn't his fault either. How far does the blame go? Does it extend all the way to conversations my parents should have had? Hypotheticals: *We'll drive you.*

I can see the guilt in my father's eyes: *I should've been stricter, should've been looking for signs, should've thought to address this subject.* I get it. It's regret over things he never thought twice about before, but can't stop overanalyzing now. There are no solutions. This is just our life now. Some wounds don't heal; they aren't supposed to.

CHAPTER
THIRTY-SEVEN

*H*enry calls around midnight. His voice on the phone, groggy and low and carelessly British, is the voice I missed for sixteen months, and still miss.

"I'm outside," is all he says.

I don't even bother with a jacket as I hurry out the front door and head across the street, where Henry is parked two houses down.

"Everything peachy?" he asks. He notices my pajamas and turns on the car, cranking up the heat.

"Yeah," I say. "My dad was fine. He just . . . didn't think he should drive."

"And Graham?"

He sighs at the same time that I do.

"I'm afraid to tell him the truth," I admit.

My heart beats so furiously I swear it's passing through the car, thudding against the pavement.

"Tonight would have been unbearable if you weren't there." I let the words fly. "How's that for the truth?"

I'm aware that the worst thing I could do right now is look at Henry, but I do it anyway. He smiles, and I have to grip the edges of my seat so I don't maul him with kisses.

"I was happy to see you, too," he says, "*and* I'm always happy to be of service." His smile is muted, fading quickly, and he stares vacantly ahead, transfixed on something in the distance.

"Henry . . ."

"That must've been really hard, for your dad to call you." He runs his hand over the top of the steering wheel, back and forth, watching his fingers move across the leather.

"It was strange," I say. "He gave me that whole spiel about how I'm supposed to call him if I ever think I shouldn't be driving."

Henry's hands stop moving, and he leans his head back against the headrest, turning slightly to look at me. "Had you ever needed to call him before?"

"The one and only time I've ever been drunk I was at home with Dawn in my room, with no plans to go anywhere else. We were playing Monopoly."

Henry smiles, but I catch him biting the corner of his lower lip.

"Have you?"

"Needed to call someone—yes," he says roughly.

"Who did you call?"

He hesitates. "No one." He rubs his eyes. "I never called any-one. I would just drive. And it always turned out fine, so . . ."

"It happens all the time," I find myself saying. It's like we said that day in econ, when we talked about the diffusion of responsibility—we're all more aware now. "But what were you thinking?" The words fall out, and I shake my head. I sound like Patricia Johnson, like this is a bad *Lifeline* interview. "You probably weren't thinking at all."

The truth is: I want insight into my brother, even though he and Henry are so different.

"I *was* thinking." He looks at me with stormy eyes. "Like the night of Sutton's graduation, I didn't care. All I wanted was to see you. I knew it probably wasn't the best idea for me to drive. And I did consider not going to Sylvia's. But not seeing you that night felt . . . unimaginable."

I try to think back on that night, try to remember if Henry had been tipsy. Maybe I just couldn't tell. I'd had nothing but water all night and *I* felt tipsy—like I'd had ten glasses of champagne—or however many it takes to feel like you're fly-ing. Like you're untouchable.

"I'm so sorry," he says, taking my hand and squeezing it, closing his eyes. This is what eats at him, keeps him up at night. This is what he tries to forget when he kisses me. Not who my brother is—but who Henry is, or almost was. How close he came to ending up like Jonathan.

I think about changing the night—giving back Henry. He'd stay at Matt's party; Graham would keep Grace occupied; Jonathan and Sutton would be having too much fun to leave. My mind is a blur, but if I could just get it straight, the new order of the night, then maybe I could forget this pesky feeling that's tugging at me from every angle—a compilation of our mistakes that made it possible for Jonathan to walk out of that party and get into his car.

"Amanda," Henry says softly. "Should I not have told you?"

Instead of answering him, I lean over the center console and wrap my arms around him, tighter and tighter and tighter until he's clutching my shoulders and burying his face in the crook of my neck. He pulls back and is about to kiss me—but suddenly there's a sharp rapping on the window.

I whip around in surprise. Henry's arms fall away and he leans back. It's Jonathan; I can tell by the baggy hang of his T-shirt, the only part of him I can see through the passenger window. He walks to the front of the car, under the glow of a streetlight, so there's no choice but to notice him.

Henry's stare is unwaveringly angry. It's the first time he's seen my brother since before the accident, other than watching him on *Lifeline*. I open my door and step out, leaning against the door and leaving one foot in the car.

"What, Jonathan?"

But he's staring through the windshield at Henry. I'm not the reason he's here at all.

Henry gets out of his car all the way, shutting the door behind him.

"Do you want me to see your sister?" Jonathan asks him.

Henry's eyebrows shoot upward. "No," he says. "I—I don't want you anywhere near her."

Jonathan nods. "Then tell her to stop calling me." His eyes shift to me. "Are you coming inside?"

"Yeah, I'll be there in a second."

Jonathan hesitates—a flash of my brother from before the accident, reluctant to leave me out here at night alone in a parked car with a boy. He walks slowly toward the house, looking back at us twice.

Henry and I climb into his car, but it's like all the air has left.

"I should probably go inside," I say.

Henry nods. "Yeah." He looks at me, and I don't know if I move first, or he does, but I'm kissing him and he's kissing me back; my fingers play in his hair, and he keeps a hand behind my head, holding me to him. Because outside of these suffocating circumstances and burdens that we'll never really be free of, this is all we have.

Jonathan's sitting on the stairs in the dark, waiting for me, when I walk inside.

"Not now," I say. I'm not in the mood to hear his opinion about Henry and me.

"I was warned, you know, about the two of you," he says, standing.

I don't like the way he's now towering over me, looking down at me.

"Is that what Sutton told you during your forty-eight seconds of conversation?" I push past him and start heading up the stairs. I don't even look to see how he reacts to this comment.

"No," he says. "It was Grace."

I whirl around to find him still on the stairs, leaning against the railing, watching his hands as they fiddle with the hem of his shirt.

"She told Sutton and me we weren't the real Crane-Tart love story. I always thought she was kidding." He winces. "Then I saw you with him at Sylvia's." He looks up at me. "Or I saw you guys leaving, anyway."

There are a thousand things I want to say—so many apologies they get caught in my throat. I'm frozen at the top of the steps, as he walks toward me.

"You looked really happy," he says, one hand on my shoulder. He leans in and gives me a kiss on the top of my head, before he goes up the rest of the steps.

I shake myself out of it, or try to, and follow him down the hall. It's the first time he's said something honest about that night—about Grace. I feel bad for being angry at him. But he goes into his room, shuts the door, and locks it. He doesn't answer when I knock. It doesn't matter that I'm there jiggling the handle, calling his name for I don't know how long. He never answers.

CHAPTER
THIRTY-EIGHT

*G*raham is mad, an emotion I've never seen on him before, not to this extent. He's pulling books out of his locker before first period when I approach him. He stops briefly to sigh at me, in case it was unclear how he feels about a girlfriend who leaves in the middle of a date and doesn't return any of his phone calls the rest of the weekend. He stares at me like he already knows what a horrible, cheating coward I am.

"I'm sorry—" That's all I get out before he goes off.

"I don't know how long you've been lying to me, but I'm not stupid."

"Of course not, I—"

"You wouldn't lie unless there was something going on."

"Graham, listen—"

"If you're going to sneak off with Henry, fine, but at least have the guts to tell me."

"You're right, I—"

"Instead you ditched me, left me there waiting for you, *worrying* about you, asking around about you like a moron, even after it became clear that you weren't coming back."

"It was something personal and . . . depressing." I hate that I use the word I know will work to get me his sympathy, because he'll jump to conclusions involving Jonathan and Sutton and Grace. I hate that it sounds like I'm making excuses for last night, when there are mountains of things he deserves an apology for.

Henry's a few feet away down the hall; my eyes can't help but find him. He's looking over Imogen's head as she talks to him, right at me. Graham notices that I'm looking past him and turns around. Henry's eyes revert down to Imogen in the most obvious way.

Graham's expression goes from angry to astonished. "If there's something going on between you guys, just tell me."

Graham has never lied to me, and the least I can do is return the favor. I wanted him on my side, and I still do. But I can't ask that of him anymore. "Whatever you think happened—"

"I promise you, I'm assuming the worst."

I have to look away when I nod.

"*Jesus*, Amanda." He slams his locker shut. "Who *are* you, even?" Graham holds on to his head as though it's about to fly off his neck, his fingers digging into his hair.

"I'm so sorry," I say. "Henry knew what I was going through, and—"

"That's such bullshit!" he cries. "We're all going through it! And I've tried so hard to understand you."

"I know, you're right." I'm spotty with tears, and they feel like a cop-out. He saddled himself with my pain, my guilt, when he didn't have to. I wish there was a way to repay him.

"Damn it, Amanda, I don't deserve this."

All I can say is: "It's not your fault."

CHAPTER
THIRTY-NINE

I find Henry in the art supply room after fourth period, right before lunch. It's the place we first started flirting, and the place he asked me to meet him when Jonathan was released from prison and he wanted to know whether Jonathan had contacted Sutton. It's a large, musty room stacked with shelving, piled with supplies and unfinished projects. Henry stands in the corner, surrounded by blank canvases.

He's not surprised to see me.

"So, are you okay?" he asks quietly.

"Are you?" His secrets are my secrets, and I've let some of them go.

Word around the halls is that Imogen slapped Henry, then

locked herself in the bathroom for an entire hour after she'd heard the reason Graham Sicily was back on the market. He looks to the ground, neither confirming nor denying that he's all right.

"Sorry," I say. "I got tired of lying."

He shakes his head. "We went about this the wrong way, you and me."

How could she do that to him?—it's what the bulk of the gossip floating around about me seems to ask. How does anyone go through with something knowing it's the wrong thing, knowing full well it could hurt other people? The answer isn't pretty: you just do it.

"We shouldn't have gone about it in the first place."

Henry sighs. "What do you want to fight about now, Amanda?" he asks. "Everyone knows, and we can handle them, no matter how catastrophically gloomy it is for them to see us together. I want to be with you, and now there's no reason why we shouldn't."

"What about Jonathan?"

"What about him?"

"You hate him."

"Me, and everyone else."

"I know he's awful, but he's still—"

"What do you want me to do, Amanda? Make nice with him? Ask him out to a ball game? Bond with him over a six-pack? We can manage without that, don't you think?"

"You'll just never come over to my house, unless no one's

home, and I'll never come over to your house, unless everyone's gone for the weekend. We'll spend most of our alone time in the backseat of a car, or in dark corners at parties, or holed up in here with all the paint fumes."

"I want to be with you!" he shouts. He moves in on me before I even have the chance to blink, holding my face in his hands and staring into my eyes. "Forget the rest."

His hand goes shaky against my cheek, his expression turns sullen. *Forget the rest* means forgetting about Grace.

He steps away from me and leans back against the paint-stained cement wall and closes his eyes.

I join him, resting against the wall next to him. Our fingers find each other and clasp together.

"Why didn't we think to stop them?" I whisper. "We knew what they were like. We knew what they were doing. They were notorious party-hoppers, and my brother always had his car."

I wait for him to tell me not to do this to myself, to assure me that it's not our fault, to remind me that dwelling on regret is useless, and that moving forward is the only thing I can do.

"I don't know," is all he says.

I roll off the wall and press my forehead into his shoulder. He envelops me in a hug. There's nothing else to say; this is what I need. There's no more fighting it.

CHAPTER
FORTY

That night Jonathan steps tentatively into the living room, waving an ice-cream sundae.

"I know it's flowers that say I'm sorry, but I thought you might prefer this," he says, taking a seat next to me on the couch.

"I suppose this will do." This is the first time I've ever really fought with my brother. I have no idea how to take steps toward reconciliation. I don't even think I really want an apology. I just want things to be different. "Thanks," I say, taking a bite and smiling at him, so he knows I appreciate the gesture.

"I hate that I made you cry," he says, looking down.

I'm trying to think of how to respond, when headlights from outside scatter light through the curtain openings. Jonathan leans over the back of the couch and peers out. I notice now that he's in his new, and fitted, clothes, but he also smells suspiciously like he's spritzed himself with cologne.

"Is that Wren?" I ask. *And this sundae is actually a pacifier?*— I don't say. Instead I point out, "It's late to be leaving, Jonathan." I touch the screen on my phone to see the time. It's nine fifteen. "Mumsy's rules, ten p.m. curfew."

He chuckles at this—*Mumsy's rules.*

"Gary's rules," I say.

"Oh, Gary's fine. I think he's actually sort of happy with me right now." Jonathan stands as three loud honks of Wren's horn outside summon him.

"Does that mean you're doing the Chicago Cares stuff?" I ask.

"Maybe." He shrugs on his coat.

"I won't be gone long," he says. "I just need to get out of here for a while, you know? This cage is wearing."

He's opening the door when Standard Dad makes an appearance, walking in from the den. "You're going out now?" he asks, already shaking his head as he pushes back the cuff of his sleeve to check his watch.

"I'll be right back," Jonathan calls, slipping out the door. It closes just as my dad takes a step toward it—like maybe he was going to go after Jonathan. He doesn't, of course. He gives me a small smile, says, "Aw, well," from chapter 12: "You Win Some, You Lose Some," and heads upstairs.

CHAPTER
FORTY-ONE

At three in the morning I wake up in a cold sweat. My heart is racing. I listen for signs of Jonathan. The microwave beeping in the kitchen. A toilet flushing. Shoes careless and loud on the stairs. There must be a reason I'm suddenly awake. But there's nothing. I went to sleep at eleven. There's no denying the possibility he's already home. He probably *is* already home. I tell myself to be logical and go back to sleep.

It's laughable—waking up with a start because you weren't woken up with a start. It feels like forever that I lie in the dark, listening to every creak of the house, waiting for one that tells me my brother is home safe, before I finally fall back asleep.

The next time I wake up, it's in a cold sweat again. I'm

turned sideways in my bed and my alarm is blaring. The clock reads seven a.m., so I've slept right through the noise. I'm late. I kick off the covers, throw the purple fuzzy robe I've probably worn only twice in my life on over my sweaty pajamas, and walk across the hall to Jonathan's room. The door is wide open, the bed's made. My brother's not here.

I hear the front door opening and walk to the other side of the hall. From the top of the stairs, I can see down into the foyer, where my brother is entering, wearing his running clothes, drenched in sweat, and out of breath.

"What time did you get in last night?" My dad comes charging in from the living room.

"Late. I don't know." Panting this hard, Jonathan sounds annoyed. I wonder if anyone's ever asked him this who wasn't going to laugh with him about the answer. Standard Dad's definitely never asked him before.

"You said you would be right back. You were out way past your curfew."

Jonathan shrugs.

"Hey." My dad grabs him by the arm. "I stayed up until one waiting for you to get home. You could've answered your phone, at least."

Jonathan steps to the side, and my father's hand drops.

"You have to start taking this more seriously," he says. "I got a call from Gary. He said your urine test was too watered down to obtain results. Usually that's an automatic fail, but he's willing to let you off with a warning."

Jonathan shrugs. He bends forward with his hands on his knees, like he's struggling to catch his breath.

"I mean it," my dad says. "You're still on a slippery slope."

Jonathan starts shaking. I look closer and realize he's laughing. He walks toward the stairs, so I rush into the bathroom.

When I'm done showering, drying my hair, curling its ends so people don't think I'm a slob, and adding makeup to the whole package so they know I really care, Jonathan is in his room with the door shut. I hear the shouting downstairs before I'm even out of my room. Once I'm at the top of the steps, it seems to have tripled in volume.

"You can't badger him like that. *Honestly*, who would respond well to being approached and hounded like that?" my mom yells.

"*Hounded?*" There's a banging noise, like maybe my dad slammed his hand against the table or threw his briefcase into the wall. "He's not supposed to be staying out late, doing God knows what, with God knows who—"

"He has to feel free here; it's his home!" she yells. "You can't be pushing and pushing him, shutting him in, telling him what to do like he's a child."

"He's living here for now; he can cool it with going out at night, not coming home—"

"He always comes home!" My mother shouts this so loudly I

imagine the chandelier above them in the dining room shaking, its crystal balls rubbing up against one another.

He always comes home.

Except for the night when he didn't.

CHAPTER
FORTY-TWO

I've become the kind of girl who lies to her best and only real friend about cheating on her boyfriend, who spills all her secrets except the important one: she's in a new relationship sustaining itself mostly in the confines of an art supply room, because as it turns out, several of the things Henry and I like to do together involve us being alone anyway.

Henry told me that Graham glares at him at the beginning of soccer practice, but then spends the rest of the time fielding the ball, which doesn't involve Henry, since he's still not cleared to play at full capacity and is stuck with water refill and ball retrieval duty. Imogen gave me the finger Tuesday morning as

I walked past her and her huddle of friends. I don't blame her.

Only 131 more days to go.

The riveting game of phone tag Dawn and I had been playing since last week ends on Wednesday afternoon, and I still don't tell her the truth about Graham, or what's going on with Henry. Lately, all of our conversations are like headlines.

Hot news: Becky sang a duet with a freakishly hot guy at the karaoke bar and ended up making sweet-sweet music with him in the back of the cab, too!

So true or so false: Jonathan's walking a thin line with his probation and could be headed back to prison anytime? So true!

Latest fashion trend: Dawn was last seen sporting a green jersey dress, studded gladiator sandals, a gunmetal watch, a drink in one hand, and a Delta Sig on each arm!

I don't like how she's turned our real-talk into punch lines. It feels less like confiding in each other and more like a competition for whose life is more shocking—even though I don't want my life to be shocking, especially not to the one person who's supposed to know everything about me. But lately, it's like my ability to shock and awe is what makes me worth speaking to—now that her life is all about the beach and frat parties and fake IDs and strawberry daiquiris and trips to Los Angeles and surfing and tanning at the rooftop pool of the Canary Inn. With her ocean-breeze weather and her new friends and new freedom.

I can just hear it. *Breaking scandal: Amanda's hooking up with Henry in the art supply room; if those paint canisters could talk, indeed!*

So I don't say anything as she rattles on about the gargantuan frat houses at USC or the models doing coke in the bathroom of Club Whatever, or the two-story beer bong the guys on the fourth floor made that they're gearing up to test out this weekend. I console her about another definitely-probably failed quiz, and then we hang up.

In truth, it makes me jealous that she can collect the pieces of her life so easily, while I have to hold mine together with all its cracks as it trembles beneath my fingers, threatening to break apart.

THURSDAY, 8:38 P.M.

The conversation I want:

Me: Dawn? Remember how I told you about Jonathan's drug test? Well, instead of sending him back to jail, Gary's making Jonathan get started on his community service right away. He's speaking at my school on Monday—as in, in four days—when Chicago Cares comes back *again*, staking claim on the month of November as Drunk Driving Awareness Month, even though everyone knows November is for lung cancer and April is for alcohol. They're kicking off their tour of twenty-five high schools in Illinois (marking the only time this year my brother will be permitted to leave the zip code). It's like, they booked Jonathan Tart, so they can make up whatever holiday they want and funding for travel is suddenly approved. I know I can skip the event, that's fine. But no one else will. And then I'll have to spend my remaining 127 days dealing with the aftermath of whatever he decides to say.

Dawn: [Lots of invaluable advice topped off with a funny story about dorm life that will make me laugh as well as highlight how much I'm going to love it there.]

The conversation I get:

Me: Dawn? What? It's too loud, I can't hear you. Call me back later, okay? Okay? Bye—

Dawn: [muffled]

CHAPTER
FORTY-THREE

I feel like I should warn Henry when I see him Friday morning. But he's already heard—everyone has. *Jonathan Tart for Chicago Cares.*

"There's nothing to say about it," he tells me before school as a hundred eyes pore over us as we walk down the hall.

After lunch, I stand at my locker reviewing notes one last time before the test next period, when my phone starts vibrating. I check it, feeling an unwelcome surge of hope that it's Dawn calling.

Jonathan.

I slide my finger across the screen to answer the call, leaning into my locker, like this will hide that I'm on my phone.

"Hello?"

"You answered!" Jonathan's voice is loud and exuberant. I haven't heard him sound like this since the night of the accident. "I'm downtown." Now that he's not yelling, his words sound heavy. "At the Riverwalk, by the docks."

"What's wrong?" *Something* must be for him to call me in the middle of the day, sounding like he's on a bender.

"Oh." He laughs. "Nothing, nothing. We just need a ride."

"We? Are you with Wren?"

"I'm with Sutton. Can you come get us?"

"Yes," I tell him, too stunned to say anything different. I don't know what else to do; he knows I'm in school and he still wants me to come. "I'm going to leave now, okay? Just don't— don't move."

He's laughing as I hang up the phone.

I scan the halls for Henry and find him standing with three of his friends.

I tap him on the shoulder. "Hey, can I talk to you for a second?"

"Of course." He nods good-bye to his friends and joins me by the wall. I grapple for the most political way to say this—a lighthearted opening, maybe, *so, we've got trouble*—but in the end I just blurt out, "Jonathan and Sutton are together at the Riverwalk."

Henry stands up straighter, it's like a reflex. *"What?"*

"They sound like they're . . ."

Henry's chin juts out, he's shaking his head, gritting his teeth.

"They need a ride," I finish.

"I'll take care of it," Henry says, though he doesn't look at me. He tugs on his collar like his shirt is choking him.

"No—Henry, I'm the one they called."

"You're the one *he* called, you mean."

"Yes," I say, my voice rising. "He called *me*."

Henry stares at me, and I look him right in the eyes. I won't back down.

"Fine. I'll drive us," he says.

"If you want." But part of me wishes I hadn't told him.

It doesn't take us as long to get to the Riverwalk as I thought it would. We spot them toward the end. Henry pulls into a No Parking zone, leaving the car with the front wheel slightly over the curb and the hazard lights on.

Jonathan's sitting on a bench surrounded by crisp brown grass next to a tree with a few dry leaves that are barely hanging on against the breeze. Sutton is leaning against him with her eyes closed. She has both of her crutches today, propped up against a tree. It's a clear day, not a cloud in sight. Jonathan and Sutton are both bundled up—winter coats, beanies, gloves. Like maybe they'd planned to be outside.

"What's wrong with her?" I ask. Now that I'm closer, Sutton looks like she's asleep. She's perfectly still and doesn't even react to the sound of my voice.

"Relax, she's still breathing," Jonathan says. His eyes are bloodshot. He frowns slightly when he sees Henry approaching.

"Did you bring our chariot?"

I nod and point behind me stupidly.

Henry crouches down in front of Sutton. "You got her drunk?" he says, sharp and astounded.

"It's fine." Jonathan scoots up, sliding Sutton's arm around his neck. Her head dips forward. "I've got her," he insists.

Now I can smell the alcohol coming off them. There's a bottle of vodka perched on Sutton's lap. It falls to the ground once Jonathan's got her standing. He's holding her up by her waist, and her head flops back on his shoulder, exposing her neck. If he doesn't change position, she's going to slide through his grip.

"Here." Henry puts one arm behind Sutton's back and the other under her legs and lifts her out of Jonathan's arms.

"I said, I've got it." But Jonathan does nothing to prevent Henry from taking her.

Sutton starts coughing and squirming once Henry's holding her. He lowers her to the ground. I put an arm under her head, so it lands gently as Henry lays her on the ground. Her eyes pop open as soon as she's down, but she struggles to form an expression. It's like she's not even there. I can't remember her ever being this drunk before.

"You're going to be okay," Henry says to her. As if in response, Sutton's body convulses, and she starts throwing up.

Henry rolls her on her side, and I pull her hair back and help angle her body so she doesn't vomit on herself. It's all liquid, so it's not as disgusting as it could be. Or maybe it is, but I'm too worried to be grossed out.

"You're okay, you're okay." Henry rubs her back. "How much has she had?" he shouts at Jonathan. His voice is strong, but it wavers slightly.

Jonathan shrugs. He bends down to pick up the bottle of vodka and holds it up for us, so we can see the damage. "Sutton was always really good at holding her liquor. I had no reason to believe this would happen."

"Mixing vodka with antidepressants and muscle relaxants would make anyone sick," Henry says.

Sutton's been too drunk to speak a million times before. Passed out in weird places like the back porch or the floor of Jonathan's room. But something about this time seems off. Even Jonathan looks sickly.

"How was I supposed to know what she's on?" he says.

There's a switch in Henry—from worried to raging. I can see it on his face. So can Jonathan.

Jonathan holds up his free hand and steps back. "Hey, man, she brought the vodka. It was all her. You know how Sutton loves to drink her lunch."

"How fucking stupid are you?" Henry says. I think he's about to charge at my brother, but he's got to hold on to Sutton. He wipes her mouth with his jacket sleeve, keeping her steady on her side. I've still got a grip on her shoulders, and her head in my arms.

"Don't look at me like that, Henry." Jonathan seems mad now, too—as mad as Henry. I wonder if it used to be Jonathan taking care of Sutton the way we are now. Or if it was Grace, and the only person my brother's ever taken care of is himself.

"Really, I'm the one who should be pissed at you," he says to Henry with a callous laugh.

"And why's that?" Henry says, annoyed.

I close my eyes when I hear Jonathan's answer.

"Amanda." His voice is dark, serious. "She deserves to be with someone who makes her happy. That's not you, from what I can tell. Not anymore."

I open my eyes and watch as Jonathan unscrews the cap of the bottle, shaking his head. He tips it back, slowly at first, and then he tilts it upward, letting it flow down his throat. He hardly winces as he swallows. Sutton vomits again.

"Hey, hey." Jonathan bends forward and taps Henry on the shoulder twice, trying to get his attention. Henry shrugs him off.

"Hey!" Jonathan says. His smile is sinister, like he's enjoying his anger. "You should stay the hell away from Amanda. I mean it."

Henry rolls Sutton toward me and looks at me for the first time since we arrived here, to make sure I've got her. He stands up and walks over to Jonathan. They're practically the same height, though Jonathan's slightly taller. I can't see Henry's face because his back is to me, but I watch his shoulders drop in a loose shrug.

"If she's better off without anyone, it's definitely you," Henry says. "Look at you; what a joke."

There's no time to be upset by what they're saying to each other. Jonathan takes a sloppy swing at Henry. Henry leans back, and instead of getting hit in the head, he gets knocked in the chest.

"Fuck you," Jonathan slurs.

Henry raises his fist so quickly I barely see it move. I just see Jonathan's head knocked to the side, droplets of blood soaring through the air, and Jonathan falling to the ground. I scream—I can't help it. Henry whirls around to look at me, and even though his mouth is turned down in an apology, his eyes are so wild.

Jonathan is on his hands and knees, blood covering his nose and mouth. It's dripping down his chin and smeared on the front of his jacket. There's so much of it that I can't tell where it's coming from—if his nose is bleeding, or his lip, or both. He coughs and spits, trying to wipe the blood away a few times before he sees that it's useless.

"Come on," Henry says, jerking Sutton up a little too hard and hoisting her into his arms. She moans loudly, like she's going to let out a scream, too.

"Come on!" Henry says again. I hadn't realized he was talking to me.

I stare at Jonathan, sitting back on his knees. Not even trying to get up. Bleeding. Swaying slightly. Staring at me with unfocused eyes.

"Get in the car, Amanda," Henry says. He's halfway to his car when he's forced to stop so Sutton can throw up again.

"My baby sister's not going anywhere with you," Jonathan calls.

Henry doesn't react at all—he's too busy wiping Sutton's

face. He takes her the rest of the way and eases her into his backseat. As soon as she's secured inside, she curls into a ball. Maybe she's done this before.

"Please get in the car," Henry says, walking past me to retrieve Sutton's crutches. "I have to take Sutton to the hospital."

"That's a smidge dramatic." Jonathan shares a drunken laugh with himself and takes another swig out of the bottle, covering its top with blood.

Henry shakes his head. "I don't know what else to do." He holds out his hand to me even though I'm too far for him to reach. "Come on. Please."

I look over my shoulder at Jonathan, tipping his head back to take another drink. He's smiling, still, but all I can see is the blankness behind his eyes—the way they looked after he heard about Grace.

"Amanda," Henry says, coming toward me. "If you think I'm leaving you here alone with him, you're mad. But I have to go now. Sutton needs help *now*."

"It's fine," I tell him. "Go. I'll be all right. We can take a cab. I have to make sure he gets home."

"So call him a cab. *Please*. Please, just come with me."

"I can't. But you should go. We'll be fine." But even as I say the words, I don't believe them. I walk over to Jonathan and bend down to help him stand. He puts one arm around my shoulders and leans against me. I hug him with both my arms—it's the only way I can keep him steady, he's so much taller. Henry doesn't say anything else. He stares for a moment, watching us, and I can't tell if his anger or disappointment is winning out.

But did he really expect me to leave Jonathan here, drunk and bleeding and alone?

The second Henry's car is out of sight, Jonathan lets go of me. "Sorry I called," he mutters.

I try to ignore him as I call for a cab. It arrives twelve minutes later to take us home.

CHAPTER
FORTY-FOUR

It takes me thirty minutes to clean the blood off Jonathan and convince him that the place he needs to be right now is in bed. The vodka is taking its effect. Each time my brother talks, his speech becomes more and more indecipherable.

My dad's at work and Mumsy is out, at the club, most likely. I'm very glad they aren't here to see this.

"Go to sleep," I say to Jonathan.

"Mm-hmm," he mumbles, turning from his stomach to his back. He repositions the bag of frozen peas I gave him so they're resting over his nose.

I take a seat next to him on the bed, pushing him so he rolls back onto his stomach. I position the peas under his nose.

He lets out a tired, sad sound. "Oh, baby sister. You're so good."

"You've got to sleep it off."

"I'm going to kill Henry Crane," Jonathan says.

"Go to sleep, Jonathan."

"I guess I can't really talk about killing someone these days, can I?"

"Shhh."

"I just don't know anymore." He sighs, and I think he's finally starting to fall asleep. "I just don't know . . ."

"It's okay. Go to sleep."

"I just . . . I don't . . . I don't know how to be anymore."

"Be nice, Jonathan." I feel tired, too, like I've just finished a sprint.

He sighs again, but I'm starting to think now that in this stage of his inebriation all his breaths come out heavy and exasperated. "I miss her," he mumbles, rolling to his side so he can see my face without craning his neck. "I miss *them*."

"I know you do," I whisper back, my bottom lip quaking furiously. He pulls at the hem of his shirt, tugging it upward before losing his grip on it.

There it is, exposed with the rising of his shirt—words I can't understand, written in small black letters above his hip bone.

"What . . . is that—?"

"Italian," he slurs, closing his eyes.

"What does it mean?" But I'm suddenly so afraid of the answer. "Jonathan?" I nudge him.

"It's fucked up that that was her favorite book."

"Which book?"

His eyes stay closed, but his forehead creases as he frowns. "She was fascinated by it. Thought it was a beautiful and dark story. We're always most curious about the things we'll never know, the places we'll never go." The right side of his mouth quirks up, noting the rhyme.

I stare at the quote for a moment longer before pulling his shirt down. "Where is this from?"

Jonathan's quiet. He might be asleep, but I don't care, I shake him lightly by his shoulders. "Is it from the Bible?"

"No," he says. *The Inferno.*

It was on our reading list sophomore year. I remember Grace saying she'd read it the summer before. She always picked the darkest stories in English class. Essays on the works of Edgar Allan Poe; a character sketch of Patrick Bateman from *American Psycho*; a diorama of the murder scene in *The Secret History*. What could have possibly inspired my brother to brand himself with a passage from *The Inferno*? If Grace loved it, is it to commemorate her? Or is this tattoo some sort of punishment, one for my brother alone, that only he'll ever understand?

"What does your tattoo say, Jonathan? What's the translation?"

He's silent, and even after more shaking, more nudging, he doesn't speak.

A few minutes later, he mutters, "Don't you dare get a tattoo, baby sister." Instantly, he's snoring.

I stay next to him all afternoon and into the evening, holding the peas against his nose until they've defrosted into a soggy lump. I replace the peas with a bag of frozen corn, keeping him propped up so he doesn't roll onto his back. I'm careful not to fall asleep. What if he vomits and I'm not there to make sure he doesn't choke? What if the ice melts when I'm not looking and he becomes so swollen and infected that his injuries get worse? My head is so clouded with what-ifs, it scares me. But I'm glad for them, even if they torment me. Because the night Grace died, all my what-ifs were about Henry, and I missed the most important what-if of all. What if my brother gets in his car and drives?

My mother arrives home around five. When she walks past Jonathan's open door, she doesn't come in to check on us, just shuts the door carefully.

Jonathan finally wakes up around seven that night. "You need water," I say to him. He stares at me blankly, like maybe he doesn't know where he is, or at the very least, doesn't remember how he got here.

"You need to eat." I turn on the light on his nightstand and prop him up against his headboard, repositioning the pillows under him. "I'll get you something."

He stares at me for a long time behind bruised eyes, still tired and confused. He nods.

The house is empty, cold, and abandoned. No sign of my

mother, even though I never heard her leave again. A few lights have been left on: the chandelier in the dining room, the pendant light above the sink in the kitchen—but there's no other trace of her. My father's still at work, or out. It's late enough, he could be home. But he's not here.

I drop some water and toast off for my brother, then cross the hall and knock on the door of my parents' bedroom. I don't wait for my mother's permission to enter, I just open the door. She's there, cozied up in her robe on the chaise lounge, watching television. In denial. Pretending nothing is wrong. If she can't see it, it doesn't exist. Her room, her bubble. All is well in here and she doesn't have to think about the rotten world outside.

And my dad, he's no better. Both of them, insisting we have our own lives, letting us think we scored independence early. Like responsibility doesn't have to be learned, honed. Instead, Jonathan and I were alone, free but struggling, with only ourselves and each other to depend on.

"You saw us—" I blurt out, my voice rising in astonishment.

Her face falls, she shakes her head—this accusation hitting her full force, like an attack.

"I didn't want to disturb you," she says quickly.

A monstrous growl comes out of me. "What's the matter with you?" I yell. "We're yours! You're supposed to disturb us!"

She widens her eyes defensively, and her legs, previously curled beneath her, drop to the ground.

"Didn't you see his face?" I ask.

The way her lip is trembling, her eyes ready to spill, I know she did. It's why she's in here—the same reason she stopped going into my brother's room after the accident. If you can't see something, it doesn't exist.

"You're not going to ask what happened?" I yell at her silence. My screaming contains the rage of all the years she didn't ask.

"I don't want to know!" she shouts back—and it's the most helpless sound. At this, her lips press together tight, her eyes snap shut.

"Mom," I say, softer now. I hate her in this moment, I really do. I imagine all the exquisite reasons most other girls loathe their mothers. *She nags me. She doesn't approve of anything I wear. She calls me over and over again when I don't answer. She grounds me for coming home too late. She's unreasonable.* All I have to hold against my mother is that she let us do whatever we wanted and we had to find out the hard way that we don't know anything.

"He needs help," is what I end up saying, as a few stray tears begin to fall.

She covers her mouth, tears sprouting in her eyes, too. "I—" She shrugs. "Tell me what you want me to do."

"Make him go to an AA meeting. There's one tomorrow at seven, at the church by that art gallery you love."

She stares at me, red-faced and crying. I wait for her to tell me that she'll do it, that she'll try—I wait for her to rise to the occasion.

"Get him some water," I tell her. "Make him a sandwich. He's sick, hungover, maybe still drunk. It'll be worse if he doesn't eat. He'll need more ice, too, for his face."

She nods. This, she can manage.

"I have to go," I tell her. Now she'll have no choice. I watch a shadow of fear, of doubt, of panic pass over her face. "I'll be back later."

"Where are you going?" she calls. But I don't stop. I don't turn around. I hear her again when I'm in the hall. *"Amanda?"*

I walk fast down the stairs, snatching my purse and coat from the closet in the foyer, and head out the front door without looking back.

CHAPTER
FORTY-FIVE

I text Henry to meet me at Hal's Diner. He's there before me, sitting in a booth near the back and away from the windows. It's relatively empty for a Friday night.

"What's happened?" he says, scrambling to his feet when he sees me. He takes me by my shoulders. I know what he's thinking; he left me in the park with my brother, and now this is how I look—disheveled and tearstained. This is how we see things now. Our first instinct is to wonder who's to blame. Our second instinct is to blame ourselves.

"It's nothing," I tell him, shrugging my left shoulder so his hand presses into my cheek and he can feel me smile. He hesitantly sinks back into his seat.

"Is Sutton all right?" I ask.

He nods. "She just needed to vomit and sleep it off, it turns out."

The waitress comes, bringing two pink lemonades. We tell her we're not ready when she asks to take our food order.

"How's your brother's face?"

"Terrible," I say.

Henry bunches his lips together to hide that he wants to smile. When he moves his hand from where it was resting in his lap to scratch his opposite wrist, I notice his knuckles are bandaged. He doesn't look at me when he asks, "And how are you?"

"I don't know," I answer honestly.

"It *was* Sutton who brought the vodka," Henry tells me.

"I guess I don't blame her."

"I do."

I wish I could be glad for this—there was nothing we did wrong, nothing we could have helped. Henry rubs his eyes. I want to take his hand, hold it in mine, say, "We'll get through this together." It's such a damn lovely thought.

"Henry." I pause, working up courage even though I feel like I don't have any left. "I'm never going to be okay with the way you hate my brother."

"I'm trying not to hate him, I swear." He shakes his head. "He makes it so difficult."

I try to think of something to say to that. I come up short.

"It's too hard for you, isn't it?" he asks. "Pretending certain obstacles don't exist; pretending his downward spiral isn't coming at a cost to the people around him, including us. Pretending there aren't real reasons for people to be livid."

"It's too hard for you, too," I declare, but Henry hears it the way I meant it, as a question.

"Maybe," he says.

We sit there in silence for a while, just the sound of nineties pop playing in the background and preteen girls laughing at the next table over.

I decide to bite the bullet and ask exactly what I'm thinking; exactly what I'm afraid of: "Do you think of her when you're with me?"

We had our first kiss the night she died. And Henry got the news about her when he was lying next to me in bed. Whenever I look at Henry, I'm hoping he doesn't remember the dark conditions under which we found our way to each other. And I wish I could forget sometimes, too. I feel terrible for thinking this way.

"Honestly, Amanda, I think of breakfast."

At that, I can't help but smile.

"What?" he says. There's suspicion in his voice and in the way he's staring at my ridiculous grin. "Is that what you think of?"

"All I know is," I say, "it's much worse being without you."

"Wow. How romantic. You really know how to sweep a bloke off his feet." But a smile is budding on his face.

"It's the truth, isn't it?"

He leans forward, crossing his arms in front of him on the table. "Is that your way of telling me that you can't resist me?"

"Henry . . ." I let out a small laugh.

"It's okay, I understand. You're pretty hard to resist yourself."

Can we do this? Switch to laughter? Pick up with our old jokes and just breeze over the last few horrible hours? "Plus," he starts, scratching his head, looking away, suddenly getting more fidgety than I've ever seen him before. If it's my presence that's making him like this, it's too late for him. "I'm pretty sure I'm in love with you," he says. He stops fidgeting and stares at me.

It's too late for me, too.

"I sort of love you, too."

"Sort of?" he says, but he's smiling.

"Nope," I admit.

CHAPTER
FORTY-SIX

The house is quiet and dark when I get home, except for a low murmur coming from the den. I trudge in slowly, unsure of what I'll find. It's just Jonathan, sitting in sweats with a blanket draped around his shoulders and his feet up. A sitcom is muted on the television. Jonathan's on his phone.

"They always said I had a killer smile." He laughs. "And a fondness for killer whales." He pauses again, giving a soft chuckle. "What's that? Killer instinct?"

I step in front of him, and his smile falters.

"Hey, I'll call you tomorrow, okay? Okay, bye."

I lean on the arm of the love seat, so I'm facing him.

"What's up?" he says.

There are dark bags under Jonathan's eyes, and his skin is bruised from the side of his nose to his cheekbone. But he seems to be finished swelling. There's a cut across his bottom lip, slick and fresh, like it could start bleeding any second.

"Who were you talking to?"

"Who do you think?" He continues quickly, like he sees that I'm not in the mood to joke. "Just Wren."

"Was that supposed to be funny? Why would you say those things to her?" *Or to anyone*—is what I'm thinking.

He licks his lips, and for a second I think he really is going to laugh. "I was only trying to shock her. It's harder than you might think."

"But . . . why?"

He shrugs. "Because girls like her are effortlessly impressed, but not easily stunned."

"I don't understand you lately." I can't look at him when I say it.

"Come on, I'm an open book. I quite literally went on TV and spilled my guts."

"Why did you agree to that interview? Give me a real answer, for once."

"It was for *her*, so . . ." He shrugs again. "And besides, they're always telling you it looks good in your case file to be involved in the community. I went the extra mile."

I'm shaking my head, still unable to meet his gaze. It's too flat; there's no concern, no conscience.

"If you have something to say, baby sister, just say it."

"Tell me what happened with Sutton. Why did you—"

"Get stinking drunk in the middle of the day? Because day drinking is our favorite pastime, and I had no idea she was no longer equipped to handle it."

"What made you finally decide to see her?" Really: *What the hell took you so long?*

Jonathan scratches his side as he shifts on the couch, wincing like he has bruises that I can't see. "Odds," he says.

"What the hell is that supposed to mean?"

"Odds," he repeats. "The odds that if someone calls you around twenty times a day, for several days in a row, you'll end up answering, and fulfilling their requests in order to get said phone calls to cease."

"What did she want from you?"

"Sex, drugs, and rock 'n' roll."

"Seriously, Jonathan."

"Oh, what do you think? She wanted her drinking buddy back, her fuck buddy back—now stop asking questions you really don't want the answers to."

But he's stringing me along, trying to put me off the conversation, like he did at the diner. He can't get away with it this time.

"She didn't want to talk about Grace?"

"No." He rubs his forehead, looking away from me like I'm as bad as a hangover right now.

"I don't believe you," I say, and he shrugs. But I keep going.

"There's more to you than the life of the party, a good lay, a good laugh. I don't believe you're going to keep passing up every opportunity to do the right thing."

"And tell me, baby sister, what's the right thing?"

"Talk to Sutton when she calls; listen to her—"

"I already told you, *she* brought the vodka."

"Take your probation seriously—"

"I'm speaking for Chicago Cares, aren't I?"

"Say you're sorry, to someone, anyone! Act like you care at all about what you've done—"

"You want a hero."

"I want you to act like a *human*."

"No, you want a martyr. You want me to sit there looking respectable in a tie, sobbing over Grace, recapping everything I did wrong, from that first toast of champagne to that last shot of whiskey, while I go on and on and on about regret as if hating what I did and wishing my best friend was still alive is somehow *noble*. Everyone already knows how I irreversibly fucked up— she's dead. I think that says enough!"

"You owe it to us, to everyone," I say, though I see his point. A girl died at sixteen—what else matters? "It's not for you, it's for them." As the last word chokes out, I suddenly feel dizzy with the memory of Henry and me outside Ludwig's. *That was some performance, Amanda.* It's a blurry line, us and them, perception and the truth; what you express and what you feel.

"It's not my job to restore anyone's faith in humanity. 'Look how someone awful can turn their life around; look how he learned from his mistakes, look how we can *all* learn.' It's such shit. People shouldn't need me to tell them that murder is wrong and jail is awful."

"What about Wren, who liked you because you told the truth about the party, and Sutton, who wanted so badly to see you even after everything you guys have been through? And what about me? I couldn't wait to have my big brother back. You don't have anything but witty repartee for us, even though we're the ones who still have hope for you?"

He breaks out in a laugh, crude and loud. "Oh come on, *Amanda*!" He shakes his head—I'm ridiculous; I'm the epitome of a baby sister. "It's Sutton who's afraid no one will see anything good about her ever again, and Wren who is only attracted to toxic things, and you—you're just as bad; seeing potential in me that doesn't exist, waiting for me to give you an excuse to forgive me." He leans back, his expression darkening. "I killed Grace Marlamount, Sutton will never walk on her own again, and here you all are, still giving me the benefit of the doubt." He throws his hands in the air, shrugging.

My nose is running, tears are starting to leak, and I know my next breath is going to come out as a sob. He's right; I can see the good in him, like they can, but I haven't lost sight of the footprints he's left dancing on the wrong side either.

"You sure do punish us for it."

He flinches, like the sight of me falling apart is too much for him. But he's still frowning, still writhing in his seat as if his skin is binding.

"You want to know what Sutton wants, why she wants to see me?" Jonathan looks at me, his expression hollow, his eyes vacant. "You won't like it," he warns, but I still say, "Tell me."

"When we got into the accident, Grace and Sutton were fighting," he says. "About me." He leans forward, all determination. "I'd told Grace I wished she was coming with me to Chicago for college next year. And that's how I said it. *Me*. Not us. I left Sutton out, because it wasn't about her. I wanted Grace to know . . . how I felt—she was more than just Sutton's friend, more than just someone to party with." He swallows hard—his indifferent expression slipping up, but only for a second. "Sutton heard. Didn't say anything about it until we were all alone, just the three of us in the car, though Grace had been asking her what was wrong all night. Grace could always tell. I thought it was that we'd graduated—I thought she was sad about leaving Grace, too." He shakes his head. "I should have known better. She started screaming at Grace; like this had been Grace's plan all along, getting close to Sutton to get close to me. I tried to stick up for her—tried to tell Sutton it wasn't like that. Grace told me to stop, I was making it worse. I didn't care. Sutton was attacking Grace—she was drunk and emotional and paranoid. That was my fault, I guess, for giving her so many reasons to doubt me." He stares down and is quiet for a long time.

"Jonathan," I say. I'm hoping that if he looks at me, he'll turn into my brother again.

But he's still lifeless. "I never would've tried to hook up with Grace. Sutton was her best friend. I'd never come between her and her best friend." He swipes under his nose, then stares at his fingers like he's checking for blood. "And contrary to popular belief, I'd never do that to Sutton either." His voice softens as he adds, "I did love her, you know."

I nod. Through his blank eyes, I'm not sure he can see me.

"I was the only conscious one, after we crashed." He looks to the floor, hiding from me, the way we were taught to hide, to avoid. "That, I deserved."

I say the only thing I can, the only thing that might bring him back. "I'm sorry I didn't stop you from driving."

Jonathan's head snaps up. "No," he says. "Don't ever fucking say that. Not you, too." He's at the edge of his seat, eyes ablaze, his hands balled up against the cushion. "Sutton wanted to see me so she could apologize—to me—the way you just did. The way you'll never do again. She blames herself, thinks it was her fault, as if the argument in the car was the reason we . . . *please*. It wasn't the fight, it wasn't the wind, it wasn't the rain, it wasn't the missing sign. It was the whiskey. And me."

"Why didn't you say that? When Patricia asked you," I shout. "For Sutton, at least. You had to know she'd be watching. I promise you, nobody will think you're a martyr just because you're sorry."

He sneers at me. "No one listens when you tell them it's not their fault. It's *my* fault. *I* did this. And I've tried to make sure"—he gestures to the TV—"that everyone knows." He stares at me, hard, directly, and his expression dims. "Really, the most devastating part of what I did isn't what happened on *Lifeline*. It's that I wrapped my car around the pole, instead of crashing into it head-on."

He doesn't wait for me to figure out what to say next. He's up, walking quickly toward the door.

"Wait." I get up, too, but I can't bring myself to come any closer to where he's standing frozen in the doorway. "What's going to happen to you?"

Jonathan shakes his head. "Nothing."

He leaves, and I don't go after him.

CHAPTER
FORTY-SEVEN

Jonathan spends Saturday in his room, and I spend it in mine. I emerge around four to find the house empty. Standard Dad is at my uncle's watching the game, and Mumsy just left, meeting sorority-sister Clara at the club for a massage, facial, and post-spa salad. Jonathan's not in his room.

When the sun goes down and I'm still alone in the house, I start to get antsy. I call Jonathan's phone three times—no answer each time. I try Henry's cell and leave a message, in case there's the slightest chance Sutton's missing, too. He doesn't answer, but a few seconds later I get a text.

She's here, he's not, I'm sorry. Is there anything I can do?

I begin to pace. I want to rip my hair out. Everyone gone, hiding, and I'm here with nothing left to do but wonder where they are. I can't take it anymore, so I get in my car and go. I drive to Starbucks—no sign of Jonathan. On my way home, I pass the church where the AA meeting is taking place right now. Gary's promise—*it can help*—is ringing in my ears. I wonder if this stuck with Jonathan, too; if maybe after everything that happened with Sutton at the Riverwalk, he thought to come here. I wait in the parking lot until the meeting gets out, in case. But when the AA meeting ends and a few people trickle out, there's no sign of my brother.

My father's in the living room when I get home; he stands when I come in. I watch the relief pass over his face, but notice that it doesn't stick around.

"He's still not home?" My voice is tight.

My father shakes his head. He motions for me to sit next to him. I curl up on the other end of the couch; he pulls the blanket down off the back of the couch and drapes it over my lap.

"I was out looking for him," I say.

"I was thinking about going out to look for him," he says. "But I realized I had no idea where to go."

"I checked Starbucks. And the AA meeting."

"Has been going to them?"

"I don't think so. It was a long shot."

"I wish he would go."

"You think it will help?"

He thinks about this for a while before he shrugs. "I went once. A friend in college asked me to take him."

"What's it like?"

"It's . . . intense, I guess. To me it was. But they say this prayer at the beginning—they call it the serenity prayer," he says.

I nod. I've heard of it, thanks to all the addict characters in movies. "Accept the things you cannot change, or something?"

"Right," he says. "I've been thinking about that . . . about the things I maybe could have changed. About the things that maybe I still can."

"I think the prayer is for letting go."

"Yeah," he says. "Well, I've done too much of that already."

"Dad?"

"I was a rebel." It's a Standard Dad way to start off a lecture—*this is how I relate, I know what it's like*. I feel a strong urge to laugh. "But I was responsible, too—and your mother, she was . . . let's just say she had her own ideas and her own agenda." At this, the faintest smile appears. "We never wanted to be like our parents, who hated and scrutinized everything we did, said, wore. We stayed out all night, went to great parties, made the usual mistakes. But our parents had no idea, and the things we did, we hid from them, knowing they'd disapprove anyway. It tore us from them, made them impossible to trust. Your mother and I didn't want to be like that. We wanted to keep our lives; we wanted to work hard and play hard, and we wanted you guys to have your own lives, too. We thought that would make us all closer. Plus, who were we to punish you kids? Your mother always said that punishment was inhibitory, it created shame. I still believe some of that . . . but now . . . I don't know. Maybe learning the hard way is the only way; maybe nothing I said would have made a difference."

I can picture my father at age twenty-four, getting married, graduating with a DDS, talking about kids in the distant future, paying a mortgage—I can see him not wanting to get lost in the world of his parents, having an idea for creating trust—no space for rules, no reason to lie.

In their perfect vision, we would learn to be independent like they were, and we'd love them for letting us make our own decisions. But our mistakes were too big. Maybe it could have worked—maybe it's not his fault it didn't.

The truth is, there are things Jonathan and I needed them for; things I don't even know how to talk about or pinpoint, but still feel like I'm missing. Or maybe everyone feels this way— like they've failed or been failed somehow. Families: letting each other down since the beginning of time.

"I don't know why Jonathan drove that night," I say.

My dad hesitates; he taps his fingers against the arm of the couch three times, thinking. "What about what he's *doing?*"

Of course my dad has noticed Jonathan's reckless behavior; what's surprising is that he's talking about it with me.

"I don't know," I say. "It's not good, though, Dad."

"What do you think is wrong?" he says.

"I don't know where to start," I say. "He's going to speak at my school on Monday. I'm afraid of what he's going to say. I'm afraid it will be like *Lifeline*."

My dad's face turns concerned, but there's something defensive in his voice. "I'll try to talk to him."

For now, *try* is good enough.

CHAPTER
FORTY-EIGHT

I don't see much of Jonathan the rest of the weekend. I only hear him when he comes in on Sunday night, dropped off by a car that rumbles like Wren's Jeep. It idles in our driveway, and from my room I listen as Jonathan runs back down the stairs just a minute after I heard him come up. I blow open my door, ready to catch him. My father catches him first.

"Where have you been?"

"You can't leave for days and not tell us."

"There are rules in this house."

"We're serious about your curfew!"

I stand at the top of the steps, hidden from view, as I'm not sure I want to be seen now that my dad is yelling. It's the most

I've ever heard my dad pull from chapter 3: "Punishment."

Jonathan stands there, tapping his foot, hands on his hips, smiling, like he's ready to pat my dad on the back and say "Worthy effort" or "Good one." But my dad moves in front of the door, blocking it.

"Come on," Jonathan says. He's speaking in a low, taunting tone—the same one he would always use on Sutton when he caught her being mean to someone in the halls. I only catch the rest of what he says in snippets. "I'm legally an adult" and "Give me a break." He ends with, "Do you hear yourself?"

I think my dad is going to crack—but his expression hardens, and he has to take a moment to collect himself. This is the Standard Dad he never wanted to be—I wish I could whisper in his ear that he's been him all along, the joke version. Now he can take the role to new and brave places.

"Call your friend who's outside to let her know you won't be going back out tonight."

Jonathan's very still, staring at our dad, waiting for him to snap back to predictable and lax. My dad looks like he's holding his breath, but he stands his ground; he doesn't move. Even after Jonathan rolls his eyes, laughs like he's mocking a child, throws up his hands with a "Whatever, man," and turns back up the stairs, not even acknowledging me as he passes. He slams his bedroom door and locks it—and my dad hasn't moved. I wait for my dad to look up here, ready to give him a thumbs-up. As cheesy as that seems, I think maybe he needs it. It's hard for me, too, watching my brother shut himself away. Before I can catch

Dad's eye, my mother opens the door of her room. She rushes to Jonathan's door, starts to knock, but—knowing better—gently tries the door handle.

She storms past me, down the stairs, and when she's in front of my dad, she shakes her head the same way Jonathan did. Then she walks away from him, too.

CHAPTER
FORTY-NINE

"**H**ellooo," Dawn coos on the phone on Monday morning. I'm sitting in my car at the back of the school parking lot, since the first bell hasn't rung yet. She pauses, waiting for me to match her enthusiasm. "Finally, Amanda! Even though it was technically your turn to call me."

"Oh," I say. I hadn't actually noticed. "So I guess I lose this round." I don't point out that if these are the rules of phone tag, she lost the last round.

"Where've you been?"

The answer is a combination of things I don't know how to explain to her. Especially the part about spending this morning having a ham, egg, and cheese croissant with Henry, and kissing with greasy lips in the parking lot afterward, and how even though it was as good as it gets being there with him, my mind was still on my brother, currently a shut-in, soon to be on the stage of the Garfield High auditorium.

"I've been around," is what I tell her.

She says, "That's lame-o," a word she never added an excess letter to before, and goes on about her weekend of debauchery.

"Crazy, right?" she says, capping off a story about skinny-dipping. "You'll see when you get here."

"Mm-hmm."

"I can't believe you won't get your acceptance letter for another few months. You totally have to apply to the same dorm as me."

"Mmm."

"I know you'll get in. I mean, your SAT scores alone were—" She's yammering on about nothing to fill the silence. The distance feels like detachment—I didn't think it would happen to us, but here we are. I can hardly find room to be sad about it, I'm so disappointed and bemused by what her life at UCSB has become.

"I don't know, Dawn. I'm not sure I'll be happy in Santa Barbara. I'm not sure it's the kind of place I want to be next year. Or ever, for that matter."

She takes this as the insult it was meant to be, as all I know of Santa Barbara and UCSB is what she's told me, and she gasps. She surprises me by crying.

Dawn's aware I'm applying to other schools, some in the

city, some in Michigan, some on the East Coast. Mumsy didn't give me an application-fee limit, and my hidden talent is writing personal essays, so why the hell not? Still, I didn't actually think I'd look at any other acceptances as anything more than ego boosters and safety nets, and I'm sure Dawn didn't either.

"You've never been to college." She's fast to continue because she knows this is the kind of obvious statement I don't have the tolerance for in an argument. "And you've never been to California." She sniffles. "Disneyland doesn't count."

Fair enough.

"You have no idea what it's like here," she says. "You don't know what it's like to be around all these new people, to have no one to answer to, to have the freedom of going to bed whenever you want and not having eight hours blocked off for school. Study hard, play hard—it's what people do here. They balance their life, but they don't close themselves off from new things, and they aren't afraid of being crazy once in a while."

My head started spinning at the word "balance." I blow up the second there's a break in her tirade. "I've always had freedom!" Doesn't she see? I have that—no curfew, no bedtime, no one wagging their finger at me if I decided to go "crazy." "I would never want to use my so-called freedom on keggers and karaoke bars!"

"Sorry I'm not spending all my time in my room on the phone with you, or shut up in the library!" The sadness fades from her voice and is replaced with fury. "Sorry every Friday night isn't a movie night for me anymore. Sorry I'm actually talking to people at parties instead of sequestering myself in the corner, complaining that it's too crowded." She pauses for a second to catch her breath. "Not every night out ends in a tragedy, Amanda!" Her anger is so explosive, I think it must have been building inside of her for a long time.

I'm speechless. It's true I'm depressing, uptight, closed off, like Jonathan said at the diner. Unnecessarily bitter, ridiculously cautious. But I have no idea how *not* to be those things.

"And not all frat guys are douche bags," she says in a small voice.

My chest is aflutter; my feelings are warring between excitement, because obviously Dawn likes one of these frat boys, and irritation, because this proves more than anything else how much I really don't know about her life there. But the desire to ask her about him is so strong, I almost forget that I'm hurt and furious.

"And I know about what really went down between you and Graham," she says. "Or should I say, you and Henry."

I sit there with my mouth open, no words coming out.

"You're not the only one from home I talk to. And nothing in high school stays a secret." She says this with the certainty of someone who really has left all of that behind her. It's real jealousy I feel now.

"I've only been here fifty-eight days, Amanda," she says. "I'm still getting the hang of it. I thought you of all people would understand."

"Dawn, I . . ." But I don't know what to say. I'm so used to apologizing; always, always, always having something to be sorry for. It's not supposed to be like this with Dawn.

"Just forget it," she says, hanging up.

By now, I know: people only ever say that about things that are impossible to really forget.

CHAPTER
FIFTY

*A*t school there are Chicago Cares posters everywhere, T-shirts for sale, a giant pot in front of the auditorium for planting "the seeds of your wishes for the future"—the whole shebang. The assembly starts after second period, and everyone is buzzing with energy as we're shuffled into the auditorium, too happy about missing class to realize what they're here for. *Ignorance is bliss.*

I spot Henry farther down the same row I'm in. Since the seats curve in a half circle around the stage, I can see him perfectly. It's the closest to comfort I'm going to get.

The same woman who spoke at the homecoming assembly enters the stage. She talks more about Grace, this time less about how she's gone and more about how she was killed, divulging details of the accident. For shock value, I think. And then she introduces Jonathan.

I hate that Grace will always be remembered like this. *For* this. Associated with a car accident that should have been prevented. The words "died instantly." My brother. *Lifeline.* Smokey the Bear. And now, this speech.

Jonathan comes to the stage. No one applauds, though I notice a few people looking around, like they aren't used to silence after a speaker introduction. Jonathan's in jeans and a T-shirt. The jeans are new, and they fit. The shirt is an old one, and too big, but it's one of his favorites. Light blue—like his eyes—with *The Rolling Stones* written four times across the front. He raises the mic before he starts.

"My name is Jonathan Tart. I'm only here because my probation officer forced me to be here. And because this makes my baby sister nervous, and I still get great pleasure in annoying her."

A joke. And people actually laugh, a little.

"But now that I'm standing here, I think I should have listened to her. This is uncomfortable as hell. I used to love a crowd. Now I want you all to have rocks, and I want you to throw them. Because honestly, that would hurt less."

He looks away from us for the first time. But not for long.

"I'm not going to pretend you guys don't know what I'm talking about . . . you knew her . . . some of you . . ."

Jonathan looks around at us all, not leaving anyone out.

"So I could tell you how much this sucks, how horrible

prison is, how probation feels just as shitty, and waking up every day is even worse. But this is a ride you've got to try for yourself."

His scanning eyes stop right on me.

"So do it."

Someone in the crowd gasps. It would go unnoticed if it weren't so completely silent otherwise. Gary stands up from where he was sitting beside the Chicago Cares woman. I didn't even notice him before.

"Get wasted. Whiskey is what I'd recommend. And you'll know you've had enough of it when you're having so much fun, you'd rather die than go home. That's when you should pile all the people you love into a car and drive the way you think you always do."

Jonathan's cold eyes stay focused on me.

"Russian roulette—it's just like that, just as thrilling. Pull the trigger, and let your trip begin."

He leans in to the mic.

"And then one of you assholes can be up here instead of me."

The room has gone perfectly still. I don't think any of us is breathing.

"Thank you."

He walks away, quickly stepping to the side of the stage, then down the short staircase leading to the auditorium. He walks out of the closest doors, Gary trailing after him, the Chicago Cares woman standing there with her mouth hanging open.

Henry's looking over at me; his hand is over his mouth. The crowd is a mash-up of so shocked they might laugh and so appalled they might cry. A lot of eyes are on me, a lot of them purposely looking away, some of them still searching the crowd. Graham's a row behind me, a few seats down. He's chewing on his bottom lip, leaning forward like he wants to rush over to me, even now. I try to look strong for him.

I shift my gaze back to Henry. He's still staring, but now he uncovers his mouth, straightens up. Then he shrugs. He says something. Maybe, *What was that?* Or, *That's that.* I think he might be trying for a smile.

There's nothing for me to do but shrug back.

At least Jonathan was unforgettable.

CHAPTER
FIFTY-ONE

The day can't be over fast enough, another one of those days where eyes seem to turn away from me, and in sixth period Henry rubs my shoulder, as if Jonathan's speech affected me alone. He's not surprised that I want to rush home the second sixth period is over.

Once I'm home, I try to find Jonathan. The house is empty. It's barely two p.m., so maybe he went somewhere with Gary afterward. Maybe to lunch, and he's still out.

I call him anyway, and he answers, but as soon as I hear his voice on the phone, I know what he's been up to.

Celebrating.

It takes me three tries to understand through the background

noise, and his heavy and distracted voice, that he's at some Irish
pub near the freeway.

"I'm coming to get you," I say.

"To join me!" He's cheering when I hang up.

I drive downtown, following the directions on my phone. I
park in a Loading Only zone but figure it will be fine, since I'm
just going to grab Jonathan and leave. There's a big green four-
leaf clover marking the bar—I'm parked on the opposite side
of the street. I try to call Jonathan to tell him to come outside,
but his phone goes straight to voice mail. I try again and again,
as I walk down the sidewalk, until I'm directly across from the
bar. Worst-case scenario, I'll have to go inside. Maybe this will
be possible, since they let Jonathan in and might be the type of
establishment that doesn't bother checking IDs.

I'm still across the street with my phone pressed to my ear
when I see him stumble out of the bar with Wren and another
girl tucked under his arms. His head is jutting forward like it's
too heavy to hold up straight. I start to call his name but stop
myself in case he barrels toward me, crossing the street without
looking.

He unlatches himself from the girls, and I worry he's going
to fall. He staggers slightly, catching himself by gripping the top
of a bright-yellow Porsche parked on the street. I'm waiting for
a small line of cars to pass before I can cross, but I keep my eyes
on Jonathan. He's rapping on the car with his open palm and
frowning. I think he must be insulting the car. Wren is cracking
up, leaning into her friend—for a second, they remind me of

Sutton and Grace. Then Jonathan's hands are no longer visible on the top of the car. He's leaning back slightly, and his smile is relaxed. The girls are laughing harder now. It takes me a second to understand what's going on—he's peeing on the Porsche.

The street is clear, and I could make it to his side in a few seconds if I ran. But I'm mortified. I edge off the curb a little, readying myself to snatch him as soon as he's finished. I glance around so I don't have to watch him, but can still see him in my peripheral vision.

Just a few feet away, I see two police officers coming around the corner. They're walking their bicycles, probably not expecting anything eventful to happen in the middle of the day. I think that maybe they'll laugh when they see him. Jonathan seems to think this, too, because even though he's quick to zip up his pants and step away from the car, he smiles at them, shrugs, says something to them, laughing—maybe even tells them a joke. They don't laugh, though, as they park their bikes and move toward Jonathan.

Jonathan panics. He turns around, ready to run, but trips over his left foot in the process and bumps into Wren, taking down both her and her friend. By the time he gets back up, the officers are on him. They push him against the Porsche, bending him over the hood as they put handcuffs on him. Wren and her friend are talking fast, and loudly, though they're arguing over each other so I can't really make out what they're saying. One officer stands between the girls and Jonathan, acting as a barricade, finally saying something that makes them go silent.

Jonathan's lips are moving fast—he's trying to talk his way out of this. When the officer holding him straightens him up and the other one starts talking into his radio, Jonathan begins to panic again. He's still talking quickly, but now he's shaking his head at them. His eyes squint shut, defeated, as the officer holding him reaches into Jonathan's back pocket and digs out his wallet.

A police car with its lights off leisurely rounds the corner and pulls up at the curb in front of Jonathan. As his eyes follow the car, they find me.

"Amanda!" He shouts my name over and over again. His face is alight, full of hope. Like he really thinks I can help him.

"That's my baby sister—she's here to get me. She'll take me home—" I can't hear or decipher everything my brother is telling them. But all four cops, the two on the bikes and the two that have just arrived with the car, stare back at me. Waiting. Maybe I really can stroll across the street and take my drunk brother off their hands. Promise to put him to bed and keep him hydrated. Laugh with them about the ridiculousness of the entire situation. Maybe they'd be perfectly happy to send him home safely, save themselves the trouble of paperwork and a trip back to the station.

"Come here, Amanda, tell them!" Jonathan's slurring, but his voice still carries.

I try to shout back, but I can't. I can't stop thinking about the gin rickey. The diffusion of responsibility. Henry's face when he confessed he shouldn't have been driving us. My father standing outside Newton's. My mother, holding on tight to her no-curfew policy. All the trouble Graham goes through before he drinks. The lies Sutton tells herself.

And then I think of Grace.

Jonathan's face is strained now, and the cops seem to have given up on me. They're pulling him toward the cruiser. He resists, leaning away from them, practically making them drag him. He never stops screaming my name.

I turn around, start walking back to my car. And even though my brother is calling for me, louder by the second, I manage to get in my car and turn on the engine. My hands are steady, but my insides feel like they're jumping, and all I want to do is put my head down and cry. As soon as the police car drives away with Jonathan securely in back, I rest my forehead on the steering wheel and take a deep breath. Tears stream fast down my cheeks, and I cover my mouth to keep the sobs in. But it doesn't work. I can't stop thinking that maybe I've failed him again. It's hard to be alone with myself, with all of these thoughts.

And then I remember, I don't have to be. I take out my phone, holding it close as I dial. I wipe away my tears as I listen to the phone ring three times before I get an answer.

"Dad." I'm trying to make my voice sound normal, but it's a wasted effort.

"Amanda?" He sounds immediately rattled. "What's the matter?"

I tell him everything. And when I'm finished, he doesn't hesitate, he just says, "Don't move. I'll be right there." He hangs up before I have the chance to protest or ask him what we're going to do about Jonathan.

From: TartA12345@gmail.com
To: Dawn Horner [mailto:DHorner@ucsbemail.edu]
Sent: Thursday, November, 20, 3:00 p.m.
Subject: Again

I do not blame you for not answering my phone calls, nor do I blame you for the reply text you sent—*I don't need this*—when I texted you an apology with a "but." I take back the *but things have been really hard.*

That's no excuse. Because as Gary says, there are people in your life meant to push you and those who are meant to match you (it's true my brother's probation officer is very wise; if only Jonathan would notice, he'd learn a lot). And I think you and I have always been matches; so when we were separated by distance and in different physical places as well as in different stages of our lives, we were so used to being in sync that we stopped trying to understand each other. I feel I know too well by now that understanding each other is not effortless, and I'm sorry our friendship had to be damaged in the process.

We can talk more about this (face-to-face!) when you're home for Christmas next month. It's a bummer you won't be back for Thanksgiving, but I understand how expensive it is for plane tickets when you can only be here for a few days. Until then I'm around via email, text, and phone.

Oh, and I'm sorry I didn't tell you about Henry. I treated it like a shameful secret, because I'm so used to shameful secrets. But I'll tell you more about that when you get here. Or maybe you can just see for yourself.

Also, Jonathan might be in jail when you get here. Earlier this week he was taken into protective custody for being drunk and disorderly. Oh, and for peeing on a Porsche. It's a long story, but it seems all his get out of jail free cards have been used up. He'll be headed back to the big house right before Christmas. Gary still isn't convinced they'll put him away for the rest of his probationary period, and wouldn't you know it, our lawyers are at it again, though Gary and high-priced attorneys can do only so much. Jonathan's got to do the rest.

I miss you and am counting down the days until I can see you.

Your very sorry best friend,
Amanda

CHAPTER
FIFTY-TWO

I sit next to Jonathan in a frozen yogurt shop Thanksgiving weekend, watching my butter pecan turn into a puddle. It was hard to convince him to come here with me.

We haven't said a word to each other since we left the house.

"They're late," he finally says. "Maybe we should take the hint."

I don't dignify this with an answer. It was Gary who thought it would be a good idea to do a sit-down with Sutton and Henry. Since Sutton is still trying incessantly to get in touch with Jonathan, and Henry and I are "what we are," Gary told us it would be an excellent opportunity for us to all have a "real conversation."

"A chance for Jonathan to talk about Grace and what happened, with people who care about him and know the situation.

"And before Jonathan's scheduled to go back to jail," he added, turning to me, so I'd remember that time is of the essence. As if I'd forget.

The word *closure* was also used. Jonathan doesn't believe in closure. He believes that by condemning himself, he's actually freeing himself, and freeing us, too. I don't know how to argue with him about that.

But Sutton deserves more.

"We're being stood up, baby sister," he says, nudging me with his elbow. We're sitting next to each other in the booth, because I think the best seating arrangement is not one where Jonathan sits next to Sutton, and definitely not one where Jonathan sits next to Henry.

I glance at my phone again to see if I've missed a call from Henry.

"They'll be here." Though the truth is, I don't know. Henry seemed almost as against coming here, doing this, as Jonathan. They both agreed to come here only out of their love for Sutton and me.

"That's a lot of faith you have in Henry." Jonathan says it like he's scolding me, as he lifts my spoon and watches the liquid glob away slowly. He declined a bowl of his own. I take that as a good sign—he's too nervous to eat.

Jonathan and I glance at the same time at the front of the frozen yogurt shop, the smudgy windows giving us a view of the parking lot. It's raining outside, so besides an old man sitting at one of the round tables in the corner doing a crossword, we're the only ones here.

Jonathan clears his throat as the small bells on the door chime and Sutton and Henry walk in. We wave at them as they come toward us; Jonathan even smiles. Sutton slides into the booth while Henry props up her crutches and closes their umbrella. He can't look at Jonathan, which means he doesn't really look at me either. He's gone quickly, up to the counter to place an order.

"This is London weather," Sutton tells us, scowling as she slips her coat off her shoulders. She's pretty dry, since Henry held the umbrella for her, but she still has small droplets gathering at the front of her hairline. She tries to shake them off. Jonathan hands her a napkin from the dispenser at the end of the table. He's smiling when he gives it to her, and she finally lets herself smile back before she starts dabbing.

"I hope you weren't waiting too long." Probably the most polite thing I've ever heard from Sutton.

"Oh, you know me," Jonathan says as both of their eyes glance to the puddle of slush my frozen yogurt has turned into. "Always fashionably early."

And they laugh, the way they used to, at something small and silly. I feel embarrassed and queasy all at the same time at the reminder of them together over a year ago and awareness of how unnatural it feels for them to be like that again.

It's a relief when Henry comes back, toting a bowl of

peppermint for Sutton and a bowl of vanilla for himself. He's soaking wet, but he doesn't bother taking off his dripping jacket. I think it's a statement. He's not going to be here very long, so there's no reason to get comfortable.

"Sorry we're late," Henry says, and no one answers him. "And sorry about . . ." He doesn't have to finish. We all know he means the fight, bruises still showing faintly on Jonathan's face.

"Just doing what you had to do, I guess," Jonathan says, not being discreet about rolling his eyes.

Henry takes his first bite of frozen yogurt, I assume as an attempt to contain himself.

"Boys are such heathens," Sutton says. I think she must be talking to me, the only other non-boy here, but her eyes stay locked on Jonathan.

Jonathan looks away, taking my frozen yogurt and stirring it with purpose.

"So, how's this supposed to go?" Jonathan asks.

I glance at Sutton, but she looks unmoved.

"It's just . . . it's not *supposed* to go a certain way," I say. I glance at Henry for support, but he's not looking at me; his scowl rivals Sutton's in intensity. "Just talk."

"To Sutton," Henry adds, and the reaction that follows— another eye roll from Jonathan, a deep sigh from Sutton—makes me realize that this could very well be the worst idea ever.

"If this is supposed to be your chance to grill Sutton and me about being in the same room together with a bottle of vodka, well, worry no more—it won't happen again," Jonathan says.

"Don't you have anything else you'd like to say . . . ?" Henry says.

"Plenty. But nothing that's appropriate to say in front of my baby sister."

Sutton lets the spoon linger in her mouth a second longer after she takes a bite; I suspect this is to hide how badly she wants to smile.

"Seriously . . ." Henry sighs.

"Jonathan—" I start.

"Sutton knows how it is with us." It's intimate the way Jonathan says it, his voice low, his stare fixed on her. He looks to Henry, and goes cold. "Don't sit here and pretend this is really about me and Sutton."

"You're right," Henry says. "It's about you."

"It's about *you*, man," Jonathan says, ticking his finger back and forth at Henry and me. "Because you're mad at me, and it's affecting how you feel about her."

"That's not exactly—"

Jonathan cuts him off. He turns in the booth so he's facing me. "There'll be someone better, someone who won't hold me against you—"

"Right, then." Henry lets go of his spoon and lets his hand fall to the table with a thud. "I only agreed to this because you don't return any of my sister's phone calls, and I thought that maybe, with Amanda here, you'd show her the respect you should have shown over a year ago by having a real conversation with her—"

"That's enough, Henry. Shit," Sutton says.

"You don't know what you're talking about," Jonathan says to Henry.

"Why not say something about Grace?" Even Henry's eyes widen when her name flies out of my mouth. I've got glares all around: *Too soon*, from Henry. *How dare you*, from Sutton. *I warned you*, from Jonathan.

"There are some things only Sutton and I understand," Jonathan says.

But I don't know what Sutton understands and what she doesn't; if she knows that his behavior in public, crass and unforgivable as it is, is partly, maybe mostly, for her—so she'll stop fixating on all the ways she thinks she's to blame. I don't know if he's ever actually explained it to her, even in the roundabout way he attempted to clue me in. And sometimes, it doesn't matter what anyone tells you to think or feel, your own mind and heart will decide for you and make an inarguable case against any sort of logic or reason.

I take a quick swipe at my eyes. Here, now, is not the time or place for me to cry, but I don't try to hide my tears.

"Hey." Jonathan's hand is on my shoulder. "I told you this was a bad idea. It's okay, let's just go."

"That's a great solution. Just brilliant," Henry says. But he's the one who leaves, walking away from his frozen yogurt and Sutton and me. The door swings back and forth with a squeak, letting in a short rush of outside traffic noise.

Sutton seems unaffected, staring down into her frozen yogurt dish, stirring it, lifting a small spoonful to her mouth.

As I stand to go after him, Jonathan grabs my hand. "Don't," he says. "You shouldn't go after him when he's upset."

Maybe Jonathan is looking out for my best interests, but I can see something else in his pleading eyes. He's afraid. He doesn't want to be alone with Sutton.

I tug my hand away and ignore Jonathan when he yells, "Hey." I know Henry won't abandon Sutton here, but I still walk quickly.

Henry's standing with his back to the large windows. He has his keys out, and his grip around them is tight.

"Let's go for a drive?" I say.

I can't tell if he's surprised to see me when he turns around. It's still raining, but not very hard. There's more of a mist in the air. I have the stupidest urge to grin at the way it's left small drop-lets clinging to Henry's hair.

"I'm not going anywhere." His voice is deadpan. "I would never just take off on her like that." He glances over his shoulder, then turns toward the windows. "I wouldn't do that to you either."

I position myself in front of him, close enough to touch him, but I don't. His eyes are locked on the scene behind me. I step to the side, standing next to him so I can see what he sees. Sutton and Jonathan. Jonathan's talking fast, still managing to smirk, and Sutton's nodding, looking down every once in a while, and not really smiling back. Out of nowhere, she laughs so hard her eyes close, and she's covering her mouth, leaning forward as her other hand smacks once against the table. Jonathan's laughing now, too, but his lips are still moving, talking.

"What do you think could possibly be so funny?" Henry asks.

"I don't think we'd get it."

Henry doesn't answer right away. "Probably not," he finally says.

I take his hand.

Staring at Jonathan through the dingy windows, I know there'll always be a divide. I know there'll be a lot I'll never understand. Generally after someone says I'm sorry, there's an exchange in forgiveness. Or there's closure, plain and simple. But we don't always get that. We learn the hard way. We do the wrong thing. We pay for it. We regret. We cry. We try to make it up to people. We punish ourselves. We lose, again and again.

"Amanda," Henry says. He lets go of my hand to wipe the single tear that weaseled its way down my cheek. "Remember when I said there was an exact moment when I knew I liked you?" I nod.

"The more I think about it," he continues, "I can't choose one."

This is the best thing he could've said to me, telling me that the way he feels about me isn't an isolated incident. I picture a whole cluster of moments, stacked up tall and strong. I wrap my arms around him, so tight it's like I'm trying to feel every molecule of him against me. He holds me just as firmly, bowing his head so his cheek presses against my temple.

We both jump at a loud pounding sound, and turn to see a

white streak of frozen yogurt sliding down the window.

Sutton's laughing, shaking her head, and Jonathan's motioning for us to step away from each other, a good-humored frown playing on his lips. I lean into Henry, shaking against him with laughter. He's laughing a little, too.

It's an almost miracle, I think, that things can change so horrifically—that we can be the cause of that change—and we still manage to live with ourselves, to live with one another. An even bigger miracle is the ways we find to cope with our own brutal mistakes and accept them, especially when there's no solution. Maybe, when there's no repairing what we've wrecked and we have to navigate around the sharp, broken parts of our own destruction, that's when we need one another the most.

CHAPTER
FIFTY-THREE

*M*y brother's tattoo, translated, says, "There is no greater sorrow."

It's plucked from the verse: "There is no greater sorrow than to be mindful of the happy time in misery."

He lets me in on this secret mere minutes before he's about to step through the prison doors. Again. This time he won't be coming home for three years.

"I don't know what to say," I tell him.

He doesn't smile. "Neither do I."

"Good-bye," I offer.

But he's silent as my parents hug him, and Gary leads him through the doors back to jail.

"Wait—" Panic hits me all at once. My dad catches my hand as I step forward.

I want to scream. *What's going to happen to you?*

Jonathan glances over his shoulder once, before the door falls shut.

It's the late afternoon when we get back. There are two shadows sitting on the front steps, backlit by a gray sunset. I'd been texting with Dawn and Henry the entire ride home, and here they both are, standing up and coming toward me as I get out of the car and rush up the walkway.

I hug Dawn, even though it's Henry who looks like he could use the hug. He nervously scuffs his toe along the pavement, marking a line in the snow dusted on the walkway after shoveling. He's holding a pink box that I suspect contains ham-and-cheese croissants from Ludwig's.

I pull back from Dawn. "What are you doing here?" I ask both of them.

"You know how my finals ended yesterday, but I wasn't scheduled to fly out until tonight?" I'm nodding as she continues. I can't stop staring at her—she looks the same! Except for the tan, of course. I'm amazed that I can even recognize her after the past few months, when she's seemed like such a stranger. "I was able to switch to an earlier flight, so here I am."

We both look at Henry at the exact same time.

"*I* was supposed to be the surprise," Dawn says, smiling at him. "But I saw him sitting in his car across the street, in front of *my* house, after I got your text that said you were ten minutes away."

I nod. Henry got the same text.

Dawn shrugs. "Since we were both waiting for you to get home, I thought we might as well wait together." I don't think the old Dawn, pre-UCSB—the Dawn who agreed that I shouldn't cry in front of certain people, and who thought dating Graham was a great idea—would have done this.

"I brought an assortment from Ludwig's," Henry says, looking down again, now that my parents have started up the walkway.

"Dawn! Aren't you a sight for sore eyes?" She laughs as my father hugs her, and glances at me over his shoulder. I'm sure she's thinking about chapter 1: "Generalities." Mumsy takes Dawn's hand and gives her a cheek press in place of a kiss on the cheek, since she's wearing lipstick. But I notice she doesn't let go of Dawn's hand right away.

My parents acknowledge Henry at the same time, in the same way—by holding their breath and smiling awkwardly. My dad tries to say something but ends up just letting out a big puff of air.

"You guys know Henry, right?" post-high-school Dawn says, surprising us all.

They only know Henry as Sutton's brother, a passing face, in and out of our house to retrieve her. I'm trying to think of something to say to smooth things over, to introduce Henry as someone who's important to me.

"What's that you've got there, Henry?" My mother addresses Henry, and I'm shocked that she's brave enough to speak to Sutton's younger brother. She nods at the large box in his hands.

"From Ludwig's," Henry says. "He loaded me up with every flavor." He glances at me, gives a half shrug. "I thought that maybe . . ." But he doesn't finish.

"I don't usually eat pastries," Mumsy says.

He nods, straightening his arms and lowering the doughnut box.

"But today, I could really use one."

He hesitates, but smiles as she reaches out to take the box from him.

"Come on," my dad says, motioning like he's going to scoop us all up and carry us. "It's freezing out here, and those doughnuts are getting cold."

"He was in his car, *hiding*," Dawn says to my dad as she walks beside him up the walkway. I want to kill her. But maybe she's helping us do what we should have done all along, breaking down the tension. Maybe she's been gone long enough to see right through it. Maybe it's because she's here for only a few weeks and doesn't have time for this.

"No more hiding," my dad says, looking over his shoulder and winking at Henry and me in a move he must've pulled from chapter 14: "How to Royally Embarrass Your Daughter."

I grab Henry's hand as we walk inside, and he seems more relaxed. I think that everything won't always be so hard. Someday we'll stop measuring things in sadness and anger. Someday we'll learn how to live carelessly.

LIFELINE EXCLUSIVE: TROUBLED YOUTH SERIES:
WHERE ARE THEY NOW?
PATRICIA JOHNSON INTERVIEWING JONATHAN
TART, JANUARY, THIRTY DAYS INTO HIS
INCARCERATION. UNEDITED.
Airdate: April 29

PJ: Jonathan, nice to see you again.

JT: Is it? Really? Nice to see you again, too, Patricia.

PJ: I wish it were under different circumstances.

JT: We can't keep meeting like this.

PJ: Why don't you go ahead and tell us why you're back in here?

JT: Gross violation of my probation. Specifically, public drunkenness. Even more specifically, public urination.

PJ: After the leniency of your last sentence, why would you disregard the restraints of your probation? What happened?

JT: I never met a bottle of whiskey I didn't like.

PJ: You'll be twenty in a few days, I'm told.

JT: It's true. I'm growing up.

PJ: You had the opportunity to put your mistakes behind you—frankly, a real shot at a second chance that not many people get. Several young people find themselves in this position, back in jail, breaking the rules set forth under their probation. Why do you think that is?

JT: Speaking only for myself—

PJ: Of course, of course.

JT: I felt untouchable.

PJ: Like nothing so bad could ever happen to you . . .

JT: Like, I didn't care if it did.

PJ: That's a shame. It was a real opportunity for you to set an example.

JT: A bad example, you're right.

PJ: So why not rise to the occasion?

JT: You know, it's funny, my ex-girlfriend said something to me a while ago—

PJ: The same ex-girlfriend who was involved in your car accident? Have you reconciled with her?

JT: I'm flattered you remember, Patricia.

PJ: We have a fact-checker, if you recall? Please continue.

JT: Right before I left to come here, I told her, "I'll see you on the other side."

PJ: Okay.

JT: And she said . . .

PJ: Yes?

JT: "There is no other side." She was right.

ACKNOWLEDGMENTS

Thank you to my mom, for reading early drafts of this story, for proofreading my blog entries and thank-you notes, and for endless encouragement. And to my dad, for never being "standard."

I am so lucky to work with Suzie Townsend, who saw so many versions of this story—the good, the bad, and the weird—and always had helpful advice and hope for it. Thank you, Joanna Volpe, Kathleen Ortiz, Pouya Shahbazian, Danielle Barthel, Dave Caccavo, Chris McEwen, Jaida Temperly, Jackie Lindert, and Jess Dallow.

Endless thanks to my editor, Rosemary Brosnan, for giving me so much guidance and inspiration, for caring about the characters, and for helping me discover the best way to tell their stories. And thank you to Jessica MacLeish, for lending her brilliance. Thank you to everyone at HarperCollins: Bethany Reis, Valerie Shea, Olivia Russo, Andrea Pappenheimer and her sales team, and Kim VandeWater. Thank you to Kate Engbring and Joan Quirós for the gorgeous cover.

Whatever I write, Jeanmarie Anaya, Shelley Batt, and Tanya Spencer are the first ones to see it. I don't see this changing in a hundred years. I am so grateful for our little corner of the universe.

Thank you to the writing community for their unwavering support, especially the Class of 2k15 and the Fearless Fifteeners. Thank you to all the Northern California writers. Our lunches and dinners and events together are always so inspiring and so much fun. You are all so talented.

Thank you to all the generous readers. Shout out to the book-clubbers: Brienne, Anne, Erin, and Jo.

For keeping me sane, I send thanks to my family and friends: Jeanmarie Anaya, for listening to all my far-out ideas for this story in an NYC café, and for having the best sense of humor. Virginia Boecker, for long hilarious chats, for having the same taste in hashtags and the same brain, and for being such an amazing friend. Lea, for reading early drafts and giving Henry her stamp of approval (and insisting he was a soccer player). Rowdy, for bringing Post-its and for being the Monica to my Rachel. Karisa, for always being the right person to know, my favorite non-publicist publicist. Brittany, for calling my books babies. Kelsey, for quoting *Under the Tuscan Sun* when I was having an off writing day: "Terrible ideas are like playground scapegoats. Given the right encouragement, they grow up to be geniuses." Justin, for answering the random questions I asked during revisions even though they, admittedly, didn't make any sense, for always coming home with jelly beans, and for loving this book.